CW00665356

No Sympathy

Eóin Dooley

Android Press

Praise for No Sympathy

This book is a true exploration of self-destruction. Read it in solitude and learn what it means to truly have nothing left to lose.

—Tina Alberino, editor and cult leader at *The Dread Machine*

No Sympathy's combination of urban magic, critiques of everyday life, and a plea for genuine human solidarity that both takes on and sublates our own finitude and failings is exactly what we need more of. Can we forge new bonds of solidarity, wielding the magic of modernity to make a new and better world? If fantasy is for anything, surely it must help us answer this question. On every level a bold debut from a writer to watch!

—Jon Greenaway, author of *Capitalism: A Horror Story*

The bleakest take on wizards and magic, *No Sympathy* is urban fantasy somehow still isolated from the real world. It's surreal, yet completely grounded, and is one of the most unique examples of the genre I've had the pleasure of reading. A fascinating and philosophical journey,

EÓIN DOOLEY

set in locales around the world but tethered to none. Dooley's unique voice weaves a fresh—if sad—story about what magic can be. Dooley subverts the hero's quest, the Chosen One trope, and other fantasy staples. The protagonist may be annoyed by that, but you won't. *No Sympathy* is a welcome divergence from mainstream fiction.

—Creag Munroe, editor of *Elegant Literature Magazine*

Eóin Dooley's *No Sympathy* is a rare pleasure in the world of Sci-Fi / Fantasy: a story which the reader could imagine happening fifteen feet from where they've taken lunch, or had their morning walk. This tale of a sudden-magician and his desire to use his newfound powers for good—really, his assumption that he must do so—reveals the underlying magic of contemporary society... just probably not in the way you'd expect, what with needing to graffiti a McDonald's in the process. Theo and the cabal of magicians which take him in form a collective which we all hope exists: the secret helpers on the fringes, those who work endlessly—and expend what power they have—to make the world incrementally better. But, as must always be asked, and as all the great stories in this tradition do: at what cost?

—Mike Rugnetta, co-creator of Fun City Ventures

NO SYMPATHY

Copyright © 2024 by Eóin Dooley

Published by Android Press
Eugene, Oregon
www.android-press.com

Edited by J.D. Harlock
and Justine Norton-Kertson

ISBN: 978-1958121870

All rights reserved. No part of this book may be reproduced in any manner whatsoever without written permission of Android Press, except in the case of brief quotations embodied in critical articles and reviews.

Contents

Chapter One

We must try to become magicians, if we are to be truly moral.

—Novalis, Fragments

Theo never considered himself a vagrant, even after learning to teleport.

Granted, he had many of the canonical symptoms of homelessness—a gnawing lack of material wealth, an unkempt beard and scruffy clothing, and, of course, the absence of any fixed address. Yet, no matter how much these facts ate away at him, he denied their existence. He believed what he needed to believe, and felt what he needed to feel, as a matter of survival. Even when some part of him knew the truth, he could philosophise it away.

This contradiction came to a head one sour night at a house party in Berlin. It was a convocation of musicians, artists, and university students. Theo knew only a bare fraction of them, primarily through his time spent busking. All of them were invited by Larissa, on whose couch he was crashing and who'd just been signed to the Tresor record label. Theo probably shouldn't have been there that night, but Larissa, good soul that she was, insisted he was a housemate, same as the rest.

The party started off well. To prepare himself, Theo had sipped on a couple of *Radlers* and polished them off with a joint, which left him nice and relaxed and only a little merry. As more people arrived, however, he became increasingly walled off by circles of friends and friends-of-friends. He attempted to break in by offering to nip out to a Späti to fetch more alcohol, only to learn the guests had brought more than he could ever afford. For his efforts, he would be fobbed off with a beer or a sparkling glass of *Rotkäppchen*. By the time the night was in full swing, he'd taken to tottering around the apartment, eventually stumbling into the sitting room where he tripped and spilt a Pilsner all over Larissa's two-thousand-euro amp.

Now, Larissa was cool about most things but not, it turned out, when you wrecked her two-thousand-euro amp. Said amp, which had been dutifully streaming music, exploded in a shower of sparks, killing the music stone-dead. Theo was left swaying alone in the corner, staring at the black brick before him.

"What the hell did you do?" Larissa called out, thundering over to him.

A half dozen faces followed her march. The other half looked away. Much has been made of the German word Schadenfreude, but the language also offers *Fremdschämen*. Embarrassment at someone else's embarrassment. Not that he should be embarrassed, he decided.

Theo pressed himself against the wall, if only to keep his balance.

"Wasn't my fault," he mumbled, voice thick with drink. "You put it in a weird place. Anyone could've tripped—Like me. I could've tripped. Well, I did trip. So, there."

Larissa blinked at him in amazement. One of her friends, whose name Theo had already forgotten, ran off to get paper towels from the kitchen. His head swayed about the room, taking in everyone staring at him.

"Sorry," he said. "I have my guitar. Should I pl—"

"No, Theo," Larissa said under her breath. "I think you should leave."

Theo swayed forward, sobering with alarm. "Sorry, I think I misheard you."

"No, you didn't. This has been a long time coming."

"You'd kick me out over an amp? Don't be ridiculous. I can get a replacement."

"Please don't lie to me." Larissa rubbed her forehead. "I'm sorry to do this, but this was what, your third second chance? Your fourth? You only get so many. You're homeless, unemployed, and an alcoholic. You need to get your life in order. I can't—"

"Hey, hey," he snapped. "Those are very inaccurate insults. For one, I can't be homeless. I have been sleeping on your couch. Ergo, I have a home. Two, I'm a musician, so I'm self-employed. Being a creative's a highly demanding vocation, as you well know. Three, I am not an alcoholic. Addiction is a physical syndrome, and I lack physical withdrawal symptoms. Hence, it's a psychological compulsion, and like, obviously, mind-body dualism is a thing. Are you going to argue with Descartes, Larissa? Are you?"

Larissa frowned as she listened to his protests.

"Theo…" she shook her head. "Get out. Take your things with you."

Theo shrugged. "Okay then."

This was how Theo, with a hiking pack, guitar case, and two canvas tote bags, found himself once again on Berlin's streets. This fact didn't disturb him. He could shove any fact aside with force of will. He'd find somewhere else to go. He always did.

He took out his phone and got to work.

"Hey Hasim, sorry about the late hour. Hope I didn't wake you. Listen, I got kicked out. Can I stay at your—Oh. You hung up on me. Cool."

"Hi Thomas, how are you doing? Yeah, I know, it's been a minute. Would you—what do you mean do I have your money? We're all squared up. No, no, I'm telling you, we're square. I paid you back. Please don't do this to me. Not now."

"Moin moin Monika. Bad time? I just—I just—Let me speak, will you? Oh, well, that's a cruel thing to say to someone. That's really fucking cruel, Monika, when I just wanted to reconnect and—Monika?"

With the gamut run, he was left staring at his blank, empty phone screen.

Well, the night was warm. Theo could sleep bohemian tonight. He figured Treptower Park, a little way outside the city centre, would be a likely spot. Scouting around, he found a shopping trolley tucked away behind a public toilet and loaded up his possessions.

The cosmos provides, even when friends won't.

Theo's wheels clattered down the street in the dead hours. He made his way alongside the S-Bahn, letting the railway sounds cover him as he strolled through arcades of shuttered shops and restaurants. The silver dome of the Berliner *Fernsehturm* hung over him like a second, shadowing moon. The only others out were the nighthawks following the city's sempiternal raves. Few glanced at him. Few want to pay attention to someone who looks like him.

Theo knew this well. It's why he hated shelters.

He didn't want to look at people like that either.

His path brought him out into eastern Berlin, where the city broke open like a book. There, vast roads and sparse high rises allowed the full depth of the sky to be felt. He turned to trundle along the Spree. Eye-height billboards turned to the street art of the East Side Gallery. The remnants of the Wall stood just opposite the glittering Mercedes-Benz Arena. As he plodded forward, a man dressed in a decent suit and smelling of bison-grass vodka stumbled up to him with a heavily accented "*Guten Abend.*" Theo guessed he was Polish, maybe. The man rifled in his suit pocket, withdrew a crumpled fifty euro note, and tried to press it into Theo's hand. Theo knocked it onto the ground.

"*Yo, Alter. Bitte verpissen Sie sich. Kein* charity case *hier.*"

The man's brows furrowed. He replied in English. "I thought anybody would like fifty euros."

"Yes, well, I don't need your pity."

"It's not pity. It's compassion."

"Alright, Korzybski. Whatever. Talk semantics somewhere else."

The man harrumphed and walked away, leaving the fifty on the ground.

Having defended himself, Theo felt it was now acceptable to pick it up.

The park was vast and silent, mantled by tall trees whose leaves seemed cut from one great swath of shadow. The Spree banded one side of the foliage, and along its path, Theo spotted a pedestrian bridge, one with ample greenery which would offer shelter and privacy. He set himself down there with a fresh bottle of bison-grass from a Späti, and a bit of weed from one of the park's dealers, all courtesy of the fifty from Korzybski.

As he rolled out his bright blue sleeping bag, he told himself the day had been hard. These luxuries were thus not only helpful hypnogenics ameliorating the night, but just desserts befitting his hardships. He decided his only regret was the lack of apple juice with which to mix the vodka. He smoked a couple joints and drank a perfectly reasonable quarter of the bottle. It was downright temperate of him.

A warm, pleasant buzz enfolded him, like a hug from someone else's parent.

He got into the bag, lay down, and closed his eyes. Weed, like alcohol, had always helped him sleep. One could perhaps argue it would ruin his sleep as he became dependent on it. It was a matter of perspective, like all things, and only he could determine his own perspective. This allowed him to decide his life was good, in fact. This was all cool and Berlin and authentic. Nothing but inspiration and artistic gestation, baby.

None of this self-deception brought him to sleep. It couldn't overcome the cold, hard dirt which pressed into his bones. He remained there for an hour, willing himself to fall away into unconsciousness, but the more he tried to relax, the more agitated he became.

He was sleeping in the fucking dirt because nobody gave a fuck about him.

Theo rolled over and grabbed the alcohol. He stood up and, still in his bag, shuffled over to the water's edge. He stared out at the river's surface as it glinted under industrial light. He knocked back a slug from the bottle, hoping to muddle his head more.

He had no money. He had no job. He had nothing. He had nowhere to go.

He drank more. His heart burned from all the acid in his gut.

He kept staring at the water, the shimmering, coruscating scales of the Spree. Golden rings appeared and disappeared with each undulation. Little chains, linking to somewhere that isn't here, disrupted only by the bridge which blocked the light.

He knocked back more vodka.

All bridges were really the same, he observed. In his mind's eye, he saw how every bridge contained two halves. Above was the daylight half where commerce passes along, where couples lock their padlocks together, from which pedestrians gaze upon the river. Half a world, filled with people with places to go.

The underworld was different, yet it had its own regularities. You could count on the underside to have graffiti drawn on it, or band posters splashed across it, to smell of urine, to be littered with cigarette butts and broken glass and other debris. Homeless people sleep under bridges, dragging out filthy mattresses to lie upon. The undersides of bridges aren't connections between places but the same place, repeated over and over. Every single one of them is ridden with the same grimy essence.

Though, down here was the water. Water, which all stems from the same global system. Bridges may connect land masses together, but rivers connect every bridge to every other bridge. Bridges are liminal, but water is superliminal. This black-gold thread before Theo would lead him out to all the seas and oceans. It could carry him out far away from here. He could be as easily there in Berlin as anywhere in the world. Drift out, into the great expanse of nowhere.

The water wouldn't even be that cold.

He pulled the sleeping bag tight to his chest, the world swaying before him. As his thoughts built atop one another, with the humming energy of epiphany, he noticed a shifting in the links of light. One small patch of space, a little bigger than his fist, distorted. He wasn't sure if it had been there before. The centre was dark, and the streetlight lensed around it, forming a halo of sodium-vapour orange.

Theo squatted to get a better look, not entirely sure if this was a hallucination. The patch was floating perhaps a foot or two over the water's surface. Through it, the wild grasses of the far shore warped, though the patch itself didn't move. It was a singularity, punched into the world.

He wasn't sure if it was there at all, yet somehow, he felt it was there for him.

He shuffled a little further forward and slipped. He fell right off the water's edge.

His stupor was such that he couldn't even gasp in surprise, let alone try to backpedal or stick out a hand. He fell like a log. Yet, before he could hit the water, he vanished, leaving behind nothing but a breeze.

All of a sudden, Theo was nowhere at all.

Chapter Two

*Master Nathaniel, I'd like
to reason with you a little,'
he said. 'Reason I know, is
only a drug, and, as such, its
effects are never permanent.
But, like the juice of the pop-
py, it often gives a tempo-
rary relief.'*

—*Hope   Mirrlees,
Lud-in-the-Mist*

S hadow switched to eye-piercing light. The air thrummed with
distant traffic. It rumbled through Theo's befuddled skull, waking him from his slumber on dry dusty land. He'd been lying face
first, still wrapped up tight in his bright blue bag, with drool pooling
around his cheek.

He rolled over and sat upright. There were trees that weren't there
before, across a river darker green in hue. Past these new trees were
tall pastel-coloured buildings built in a style he didn't recognise. The

air was warmer and smelled faintly of burning plastic. He also had a headache.

At first, Theo thought he had woken into a lucid dream, though some sober part of him sensed something was amiss. An unnamable fear gripped him. He leapt out of his sleeping bag. Or at least, tried to. His feet snagged on the bag and he crashed down in the dirt.

From this new vantage point, he saw the posters on the wall were no longer *auf Deutsch*. They were written in a series of runic slashes and dots. His head bobbed and swayed, trying to take in the curves. The source of the language burbled up in his bleary brain.

"Why are they advertising in Chinese?" he murmured.

He stared at the posters as if they would tell him.

They did not.

Then he noticed his trolley was absent—the one with all his belongings.

"Alright," he exhaled. "Time for calm, rational analysis, Theo. The posters aren't a priority. The trolley isn't a priority. The priority right now is to not freak out. Let's do a judicious and exigent display of not freaking the fuck out, and learn where we are. And maybe find some paracetamol."

He stood up, dusted himself down, and dug his phone out. It had no signal but assured him he was still in Germany and, daylight notwithstanding, it was 1:27 AM. The official word of Samsung failed to dispel his concerns, however, especially since he lacked signal.

He slapped himself in the face in case he was dreaming.

His experiment yielded little fruit. However, he did feel a touch more sober.

Theo scrambled up the hill towards the bridge. His shoes slid, and his face smacked into the dirt once more, but he hauled himself up and vaulted over the railing at the top.

He appeared to be on the edge of some industrial complex. There were fences with barbed wire, suggesting few came through this road unless they had guns and badges and that kind of thing. The signs here had alarming pictograms indicating fatal consequences for either staying here or leaving here. He wasn't sure which.

"Okay," he said. "Don't run. Running is not a problem-solving strategy. Unless you're a runner, or a hunter, or about to be shot by a security team."

He shook his phone, hoping the aggression would motivate a carrier to pick him up.

"It's fine though, really. See this? This is not Mars. This is fine."

The phone confirmed his location. He was beside the Ng Tung River, on the outskirts of Shenzhen, China, which bordered Hong Kong. It was 11:44 AM. Back home in Germany, it was 4:44 AM.

Theo gave a long, low whistle. All his worldly possessions were sitting unattended in a trolley several thousand miles away. He had a wallet with maybe five euros in it, but nary a lick of yuan and fuck-all folks to call on. His Chinese extended about as far as *ni hao* and he could hardly *ni hao* his way into 'Please help me, I have been transported by an unaccountable spatial anomaly into your country. I would like a plane ticket to Deutschland *tout de suite*, and I will not be taking questions at this time'.

He wasn't even sure if *ni hao* was Mandarin or Cantonese, nor which of the two they spoke in Shenzhen.

"Okay. An inventory. Obviously, my sense of reality is breaking down. Could be cannabis-induced psychosis. Maybe the weed was laced with something. Maybe I've lost my mind. Total psychotic break independent of any drugs. Always a risk. Seems unlikely though. Maybe aliens are messing with me. Or Cartesian demons. Or a glitch in the matrix."

He hammered the corner of his phone into his forehead. "Let's assume the reality I'm experiencing is fake. If so, then I have to be calm. It's merely a bad trip, or something equivalent. If this reality is real, then I came here via something supernatural, which I can't anticipate. But perhaps I can find clues. I have to focus on what's in front of me. My body looks the same as before. I got my clothes, the sleeping bag."

The sleeping bag. It came with him. So had his clothes. If a supernatural phenomenon had transported him, it had done so with respect to peripersonal space. Perhaps he could logic his way out after all. He took heart knowing that whatever was happening, it was significant, and since it was happening to him, that made him significant too.

Theo slid back down the bank and stared at the sleeping bag. It lay ominously out on the concrete. With a decisive swipe, he lifted it off the ground. There was no cartoonish trapdoor or runic circle underneath. The bag didn't smell of any strange drugs, magic powder, brimstone, or anything beyond himself.

He struggled to remember his transit, veiled as it was by a haze of bison-grass vodka. He knew he had been beside the Spree in his sleeping bag, and he knew the world hadn't changed before his eyes. He put the bag over his head, turning himself into a giant blue cocoon, and then removed it with a flourish. Nothing happened.

He refined his theories. Alien technology wouldn't leave a smell, presumably, nor would a glitch in a simulated reality. Following the rules of Bayesian probability theory, these hypotheses were the more probable. Theo felt good at having made a solid inference about his situation.

However, these theories didn't leave him with anything actionable, so they were useless.

His eyes settled on the concrete arch in front of him. A platform nine-and-three-quarters situation wasn't out of the question. He wished it were, but he couldn't rule it out. The wall before him could be a magical portal linking Shenzhen and Berlin. It could require some kinetic intent to activate.

Theo didn't think any further about this as he prepared to run. He feared hesitation might interfere with the hocus and/or the pocus. Instead, he faced the wall. His breathing was almost at the point of hyperventilation, and he took no notice of the stranger approaching him.

He sprinted forward, full pelt, just at the moment the stranger called out.

Theo slammed into the wall. His nose cracked with a burst of blood.

The stranger sucked in a breath. "*Kabes di patin.*"

He was a tall, heavyset man in a black leather jacket. He had a mean mien, with a shaved head and a tattoo of a rose creeping up the side of his neck. He repeated something in the same language, neither Mandarin nor Cantonese, and stuck his hand out toward Theo.

Theo felt the hot rush of shame across his neck. He ducked away from the hand and scrabbled to pick up the sleeping bag, shoving his bloody nose into the cloth.

"Hey," he said, muffled. "Sorry. Leaving now."

"Ah," the man smiled. "English? Do you understand me now?"

He spoke fluently but slowly and with an unrecognisable accent.

"Um, yeah." Theo lowered the bag. "Yeah, I'm English."

The man pursed his lips and tossed a packet of tissues to Theo.

"Not the first time I've seen someone do that. Did you break it?"

Theo caught the tissues. "No. My nose is made of sterner stuff than that."

The stranger studied him with a puzzled look. Theo felt uneasy.

"Are you here for me?" he asked. "Do you know what's going on?"

"Yes. To both. Where did you come from?"

"What, really? You're here for me? Wait, are you from the government?"

The man raised an eyebrow. "No? Which government?"

"Oh, okay, that's good."

"Is it? Why?"

"Uh... I don't know. I thought maybe I stumbled onto a conspiracy or something. Something I shouldn't have. Illuminati, Area 51. Stargate. I don't know. I came from Berlin by the way."

The stranger laughed, flashing his teeth. "That's a good one, chief. It's not a government thing, though. Come, and I'll explain everything. Leave your bag. We will return."

"Where are we going?"

"McDonald's."

They left the bridge, and Theo's adrenaline spike crested down into a sort of low wave. There were worse ways to be flung across the globe. The day was nice and warm, and it could still be that none of this was happening.

Despite the pleasant day, the stranger was rather taciturn, which irritated Theo. More than that, he wore a strange smile across his face, which Theo attributed to the bloody tissues stuffed up his nose.

Theo knew when he was being judged.

"Will you at least tell me your name?"

"Gabriel," he answered, smiling still as they continued deeper into Shenzhen.

Theo had never been to China. What struck him most about Shenzhen was how, in many respects, the city felt like any other. He was on the other side of the world, but the road signage was the standard white on blue; there were shopping centres of gleaming glass and metal, and skyscrapers blocked the horizon. The architecture felt different, true. More triangular roofs, with more compact apartments. The language was, of course, totally different, yet it still retained the stray Latin character or Indo-Arabic numeral, and the people bustled about as they did in Berlin. The differences, he noticed, brought as much attention to the similarities as to themselves, which left him with a curious sensation.

The sensation reached its apex once they arrived at McDonald's. Even in China, the building retained its classic golden arches, and its menu advertised unambiguous Big Macs and Chicken McNuggets. The place was largely empty.

Theo realised what it was. He felt at once both estranged and at home.

Chapter Three

*Magic in its earliest form
is often referred to as "the
art" ... Art is, like magic,
the science of manipulating
symbols, words, or images,
to achieve changes in consciousness.*

*—Alan   Moore,   The
Mindscape of Alan Moore*

They entered the McDonald's. Theo smelled the hot grease coming from the kitchen, and froze. He hadn't eaten since lunchtime—too nervous about the party, then too busy drinking to notice. He realised he was starving, and without the means to pay for food.

"You want anything?" Gabriel asked.

"No, no, I'm alright. Thanks though."

"I'm buying."

"You are? Oh, well, okay then. I'll pay you back later though, promise."

"They have everything you would know. Tell me and I'll order."

Theo opened his mouth. He hesitated, "I really will pay you back, just so's you know. You can rest assured. I just left my wallet in another continent. You know how it is, I suppose."

Gabriel gave a genial nod of the head. "Order what you'd like."

"In that case, I'll have two double cheeseburgers with chips. Bacon on top as well, if that's an option. No trouble if it's not. Apple juice to drink... I presume they have the Minute Maid brand here? Oh, and a coffee, of course."

Theo slotted himself in a side booth while Gabriel went to the counter. He began wolfing the food down as soon as it was placed on the table. Gabriel looked at him with the same strange smile.

"So," Theo sipped on the coffee, burning his tongue. "My name's Theo. I'm from Berlin. Pleased to make your acquaintance, Gabriel, properly. Warrior of God, right? That's what the name means?"

Gabriel shook out a salt packet. "You religious?"

"No way José."

"Good. Religious people have more difficulty accepting that magic is real."

Magic. Just as Theo had predicted.

"Is that so?" he asked, trying to play it cool.

Gabriel burst out laughing, and a lump of chewed-up chips lodged in his throat. He choked and thumped his chest, clearing his windpipe.

"Sorry. I like seeing people when I tell them about magic. They always wear the same expression. Though you, chief, have the funniest face I have ever seen. Trying to act like you're not surprised."

Theo scowled. "Yes, well, the others didn't have a broken nose."

"Oh," Gabriel's face softened. "So, you did break it. You want ice?"

"No, I'm fine. Just tell me about magic."

Gabe relaxed back into the seat, "Well, it's how you came to Shenzhen. Almost everyone does it by accident at first. Do you know what sympathetic magic is?"

Theo shook his head. Gabriel pulled two chips out of their red cardboard pocket. He examined them, ensuring they were of equal length, and placed one on the tray. He kept the other in his hands.

"Sympathy is a truth about the world: things that are similar are the same."

Gabriel tore his chip, and the chip on the tray broke apart.

"This is sympathy," he said, "all magic comes from it. Every historical practice of magic uses it. Druidism, black magic, onmyōdō, whatever. They all say that having a symbol of a thing means having power over the thing. Witches can make poppets to control people, wizards can learn true names to control objects. This is the idea. Now, sympathy is the word for the closeness between things. Think of it like a thread. Everything is connected to everything else with this thread, but the more two things are alike, the stronger the thread becomes. A strong thread means it is easier to do magic."

"That's why you checked if the chips were similar."

He nodded. "They were probably from the same potato, too, which helps. The thing most similar to something is the thing itself."

"Well, the chips probably weren't from the same potato. Those kinds of chips are made in giant factories with thousands of other potatoes and all mixed around together."

"Ack," Gabriel waved his hand. "Don't tell me these things."

"Why not?"

"It stops me from doing the trick," he said. "The big misunderstanding about magic is thinking the symbols have the power. They don't. Similarity is a personal thing. It comes from how people see the world, so the symbols only matter in how they matter to you. Magic boils down to seeing two things as kin, to finding a good thread to connect them. There's no official name for this act. Magicians have lots of different ones. The one I know in English is Regarding. When you Regard, you think about how two things are similar. You think about a symbolic connection between them. This creates a literal connection. If it is between objects, you can affect both at once. If it is between places, you can move across the connection."

Theo was struck by the memory of bridges, drunkenly musing about how they were all alike. If magic worked like Gabriel said, then he had been present at every bridge, drunkenly musing about all of them.

"This seems too easy."

"There are costs. The cost for movement is time. Weak sympathy between locations makes for longer journeys."

Theo totted up the numbers to figure out his delay.

"I lost three-and-a-quarter hours," he murmured.

Gabriel's brow furrowed. "Huh. Most would lose a day, even with experience."

Theo was thrilled. Not only was he at last a natural at something, but that something was magic. However, he couldn't quite imagine what being a master of magic entailed. Still, whatever this secret world was, he knew he wanted it. He knew his moment had come, and his life could finally really begin.

"Brilliant! So then, are there other costs? Wait, why couldn't I do this before? Is it like some ancient bloodline giving me latent abilities? No, wait, why Shenzhen anyway? And why are you here? Are you—"

Gabriel held up a hand. "I'm not a local. I'm from Curaçao."

"Like the liqueur?"

"Indeed. Maybe I'll show you the island sometime. As for why I'm here, every magician comes to have a duty. A calling. Mine is I like to help new magicians."

With his plastic fork, he pointed in the direction they had come. "Over there, close by your bridge, is the Luohu Commercial Centre. It is one of the largest fake markets in the world. If you want duplicates of famous clothing, bags, watches, or whatever, you can get it there. There is a whole village not far from here, Dafen, that makes copies of famous art for it. Good duplicates hijack sympathetic ties, and famous things have a lot of strong ties. Shenzhen is a natural place to fall if you don't know where you're going."

Theo chomped on his chips in greedy thought, his leg jittering under the table.

"All this is just making mental connections." he said between bites. "Why couldn't I do it before? Why can't everyone do it?"

Gabriel licked his lips, studying Theo. "There's a catch. I'm not sure if I want to say. I don't think you'll like it. I think it might insult you."

Theo guffawed and wiped the ketchup off his mouth. "You don't know me. We just met. Besides, I have just learned magic is real, so my entire conception of ontology has gone topsy-turvy, and so my ego, consequently, is at a zero, alright?"

"Sure. Well, you do need to know this." Gabriel scratched his neck. "The one requirement to use magic at all is that you must be a forgettable person. People can't think about you."

Theo's leg stopped jittering. "What the fuck does that mean?"

"Magicians Regard other things as being the same to do magic, but they must be Regarded by the world as being the same, or not Regarded at all. People entangled in the threads can't pull on them. You have to be on the outside. Distanced. I saw your sleeping bag. I think you know what I am talking about."

Theo remembered the screen of his phone—the lack of contacts to call on.

"No, I don't know," he said. "You're talking to me right now, aren't you?"

"True, but we're both on the outside."

"Oh, I misunderstood. So, there's like a whole underground society out there then."

"No, magic does not blend with society. Too big a group, and it all goes away."

"Well, you can still teach me, evidently, so why hasn't everyone heard about this?"

Gabriel sipped his coffee. He savoured it, inhaling gently. Then he continued.

"If you learn someone is a real magician, they become famous. If they become famous, everyone starts to think about them. This strengthens the ties on them and stops them from slipping the threads. Occult is the opposite of famous. Hidden. Secret. But a little friendship only makes it harder, not impossible. It's not the end of the world."

Theo was silent for a moment. Then he plucked out two chips. "Can I try your trick?"

Gabriel shrugged.

Theo laid out one chip in front, holding the other with both hands. He imagined each overlaying the other, occupying the same space between his fingers. He felt a tension in the thought, much like before, like stretching out a rubber band without knowing its limit. He broke the chip.

They peered in at its counterpart. There was a hairline fracture.

Gabriel snorted.

"Was that good?" Theo asked. "How quickly can new magicians do that?"

"Not that quickly."

"Fuck yes!" Theo tossed the broken chip into his mouth. "I knew I'd have a knack for this. Alright, what's next? Oh, should I call you *Sifu* or Guru or something?"

"If you call me anything, call me Gabe." His teacher thought for a moment. "Okay then. We need to go back to the bridge. You need to know how to move around on your own."

The dim praise had inflamed Theo as a spark inflames gasoline, and now his mind was afire with possibility. He sensed magic was a system like any other. It could be analysed, then pushed to its limits, until its basic substrates bent and warped like space-time in theories of physics. It would be an exercise in creativity, a skill he felt he was trained in.

Forget guitars. Those were dead-end instruments next to reality itself.

By the Ng Tung, they opened up Google Maps. Street view allowed Theo to compare reference points between this river and the target river, the Spree. Returning would be the same process as setting out, only reversed and deliberate.

"You need to believe these places are the same at their core," said Gabriel. "Pick details and build a road from them."

Theo's eyes darted about, taking in the barbed wire and chain-link fence at the top of the bridge, the patchy parts of the grass, the brutal concrete. Industrial, barren, removed.

"Reminds me of a spot out by Wrangelkiez," he said, searching on his phone.

"Good. When you concentrate on here and there, you'll sense the sympathy. You'll feel the weight. Give yourself over to it. You're building a new instinct."

"Are you going to watch me do this?"

"It wouldn't work if I did. My attention would keep you locked in place. I have my own paths to Berlin, though. Text me when you arrive."

Before he knew it, Gabe was already striding off, leaving him alone with his irritation. He reckoned a great sage would surely spring for less shabby clothing or a touch-up of a faded tattoo.

Theo felt he could figure this out on his own initiative.

He thought about the bridge in Wrangelkiez. One of his first days in Berlin, right after he ran off from England and before he knew anyone else, he picked up a pack of beer and a whole fried chicken to celebrate his liberty. His parents always wanted him quiet and ensured he had no money to spend, but he had garnered just enough from busking to fetch a meal. He'd gorged himself underneath a bridge in that *kiez*. He remembered the burble of the water around him, flowing like the water here, and the warmth of the chicken, same as the heavy chips lodged in his gut. Like the bridge here, the concrete of the Wrangelkiez bridge hadn't set quite right. They both had this long, dirty bead going down them, like some fossilised tear.

The tension in his thoughts rose.

He shut his eyes, telling himself the bridges were the same. He regarded them and then gave himself over to his Regarding, to the weight he felt within his mind.

Then, he disappeared.

Theo appeared beside the place he had imagined. It was the dead of night. The same as when he left. He got stuck for a second on the thought he'd suffered some wild hallucination, but his senses caught up to him, and he laughed. Alone and aloud, raucous and free, and startling some sleeping birds.

"You magical bastard Theo. Grade-A, magical bastard."

Theo waited for his phone to pick up the signal, a grin plastered across his face.

"Alright, three hours in transit last time. The experience felt the same. So... three again? Bet I've outpaced Gabe. How long could he take to get here anyway?"

The phone connected. He stared at it.

He checked one calendar app, then another, then he googled the date, and then he pulled up news sites. All of them said the same thing. He had lost over a week.

Seven days of his life had disappeared, and there were no new messages from anyone.

Nobody had asked him how he was. Nobody had wanted to meet up. Nobody had declared him missing. Nobody, he realised, had been worried. Even those he asked for help over a week ago. People weren't concerned that he'd OD'd or been assaulted or arrested. They were happy to abandon him.

Theo had dropped off the face of the earth, and nobody cared.

He clenched the phone for a long time, trying to squeeze something out.

Whatever, he decided. It didn't matter. The absence of consideration was an indication of his newfound god-given power. Sacred objects are those set apart from ordinary life, or so the anthropologists say, so this really only befits the mysticism. When he mastered magic, he wouldn't remember this.

He texted Gabriel: *I'm here. Meet you at Treptower?*

As if the man would text back anytime soon. There was no way he would wait for someone he had just met in a random city for a week. Theo had already embarrassed himself. For all he knew, his teacher had moved on by now, so he'd have to induct himself into the mysteries.

He set out to find a shoulder of whiskey or a bottle of dirt-cheap *Korn* somewhere.

Then his phone lit up.

Be right there :)

Theo blinked at the screen. He placed the phone back into his pocket. He stood there for a moment, feeling the wind blow across him, watching the small shadows cast by the moonlight. He saw an empty beer bottle on the ground. He walked over to it, and picked it up. He wiped it down and placed it in his pocket. He could return it for a deposit. It would only be a few cents, but a few bottles could make a euro.

Theo began his return to Treptower, picking up every bottle and can he saw on the way.

He would keep his word. He'd pay Gabriel back for that meal.

Chapter Four

A magnificent life is waiting just around the corner, and far, far away. It is waiting like the cake is waiting when there's butter, milk, flour and sugar. This is the realm of freedom. It is an empty realm. Here man's magnificent power over nature has left him alone with himself, powerless. It is the boredom of youth without a future.

—Henri Lefebvre, Introduction to Modernity

G abriel spent months training Theo.

The first step was to build familiarity with standard buildings. They formed the rudiments of the routes Theo would later develop. They visited office blocks, petrol stations, chain restaurants, hostels, hotels, and government departments, all so that Theo might Regard them and hone his magic. Gabriel would have him study a target, taking details down on a notes app on his phone and snapping some reference photos. Then, the pair would relocate to a jump-off point for some trial-and-error sorcery.

The generic nature of these places was vital.

Theo quickly realised that contrary to what many might assume, the modern age has been beneficial for magic. Industrialisation and cultural imperialism ensured the repetition of the same kinds of structures across the globe. Pop culture hegemonies, factory floors, copy-paste design, international supply chains, mass media and the internet. All these were facets of a system that worked to reduce the critical conceptual distance between things. This system was Theo's dowsing rod. The facets were his Major Arcana.

However, as valuable as it was to a magician, broad similarity alone didn't cut it. The small, individual details need to be Regarded too. To move from one McDonald's to another, Theo had to note the specific wrong angle in which one tile in the corner was placed, the subtle tear in the fabric of the seat cushions by the window, the common frequency in the flicker of those failing light bulbs, or the tiny graffiti tags scratched into the table with a ballpoint pen. Without those details, his thoughts would drift within broader categories, following faulty tides that would bring him somewhere unintended, much like how he had arrived in Shenzhen.

One strategy they employed was the use of sigils. These were not runes of a secret language, as Theo hoped, but merely artificial details for a magician to focus upon. Changes they could make themselves to gain some control. Gabriel would have Theo enter some forgettable place and find a quiet spot out of view. There, he would draw an X somewhere with a marker. On the wall, perhaps, or the underside of a table. He would then Regard, and the magic would carry him where it willed. Once he'd arrived, he'd draw the same X in a similar place, which acted as an anchor to help him return. Gabriel encouraged him to develop his own set of sigils, to help him remember his routes. Through them, Theo could weave a little homespun web of locations, with different sigils connecting different spots. He went with the old alchemical symbols of the Renaissance, as it added to the general mysticism. Gabriel preferred to use the alphabet.

Such techniques were necessary, as Theo needed all the help he could get. Gabriel often had to wait multiple days as his student stumbled through his transcontinental travails. Yet, the Curaçaoan never seemed to mind. He would first find food and places for them to bed down, usually outdoors with sleeping bags. When these duties were resolved, he would turn to a satchel of books he carried, sitting down to read for hours until his student texted him. Theo never saw him read any scholarly tomes, only fiction. He was working his way through Italo Calvino during their training. His patience seemed infinite. Theo could never admit how much he admired him, nor how grateful he was that he stood by him when nobody else did.

Theo wanted to take over Gabriel's duties, to sidle up into responsibility to impress his teacher. He had him explain how he did those chores. It turned out Gabriel stole surplus food from supermarkets and cheap restaurants. He preferred to use apps that directed him to freely available goods, but he often went dumpster diving, and he was not above breaking into buildings to liberate items that had gone a bit past their best-before date. Theo was familiar with this foraging style and insisted on taking over this role. To help with this, Gabriel decided to teach him another trick.

"Is this your card?" asked Theo, holding up the six of spades.

Gabriel sipped coffee from his thermos. "Yes. Now do it again."

Theo cracked his knuckles, took a bite of his stale éclair, and shuffled the card back into the deck. Behind their city bench, cars and bikes clattered along the cobblestones of Maastricht. A sunset seeped down through the slats and spires of the city's rooftops, spilling across the Meuse River and pooling into the streetlights. It was the kind of evening where everything felt as if it was in its proper place, where one could glide through the world without disturbing so much as a breath of air.

Theo's trick required a careful and delicate delusion. As he shuffled, he took care to maintain two states of mind. One, he believed he knew exactly where the original card was as he mixed it back in among the others, that he could and would draw it from the top when he wished. Two, he did not genuinely know the card's location, and his senses were rigorously curated to avoid perceiving it by accident.

Once he felt the balance had settled, he drew another card and presented it.

"Well?"

"You have it. The six of spades."

Theo whipped the card around to look at it, no longer maintaining his belief. In the moment between leaving Gabriel's perspective and entering his own, the card changed back. Theo was left looking at the ace of hearts. He showed it to Gabriel, and his teacher nodded.

Theo had learned how to duplicate objects.

"I love magic so fucking much," he said, almost shouting. "This is the best I've ever felt, Gabe. It really is. Ugh. Unbelievable. So, you said you had a challenge for me? Something clandestine? Roguish? I'm right and ready. I'd rob a dragon if you asked me to. Show me Smaug's lair. I'll rob him blind."

Gabriel clapped a hand down on Theo's shoulder. "Easy. A soup made quick will turn out salty. Questions first. Why did the card stay the same when I looked?"

"I hid the card, so you had no reason to perceive it as anything else. Once I pulled the trick, your belief reinforced it. If you were looking at it beforehand, then it would be impossible."

"And when you pulled it away?"

"That's when we both stopped pretending."

Gabriel shook his head in disbelief, releasing him. "It's crazy how fast you learn."

"It's not hard to figure it all out. Fake it, and you make it."

"You're proud, aren't you?"

Theo grinned from ear to ear and stamped his feet. "Of course I'm proud. I'm a fucking wizard. I can hoodwink reality. Pull one over on the bloody monad!"

"Shh, or the police will put you in the drunk tank."

"Oh, right. Sorry."

Gabriel chuckled and went fishing around inside his jacket pocket. He pulled out a large keyring, which jangled with every shape and size of key that Theo had ever seen. It even had a couple of blank keycards threaded through it. Gabriel passed it to him.

"I put this together for you. Now you have your ring, eh Bilbo?"

It was dark when Gabriel led him past Maastricht's town hall into its pedestrianised zone. The narrow streets were embroidered with trees, tables, and tourists, which they wove their way through with their packs on their backs. Theo trotted along like an eager pony, trying to match Gabriel's purposeful strides.

"Okay, so where am I breaking into?" he asked. "You're having me do crime, right? I want to do crime. Is it the town hall? A bank?"

"It's the Boekhandel Dominicanen. The Dominican Bookshop."

"Oh." Theo lagged behind in thought, then bounced a few steps forward. "Is it a personal mission for you then? I suppose there's some connection to Curaçao here?"

Gabriel looked straight ahead as he answered. "No, although one of the old governors became chief inspector here. No, the Boekhandel is a challenge because it has been many different things. It was a concert hall, a warehouse, a slaughterhouse; before it was any of those things, it was a cathedral. They built it in the thirteenth century. Built for the Dominican Order."

"Oh, okay. I hoped it might be a personal thing. I'd like to get to know you better."

"Hah. What's to know? I like reading. I like teaching. I have problems with cholesterol. Are you expecting more than what you see?"

"Oh well, you know. What's your story? How long have you been doing magic?"

"Ah, a big question without an interesting answer. A long time."

"No, really, I want to know."

"I know. Here's another lesson for you. Magicians never have fun histories. It has to be this way if they're going to discover magic in the first place, eh? If you meet more in the future, and I hope you do, it's better to be polite and let it lie. I haven't asked you about your history—why you were sleeping on the streets of Berlin, what kind of family you had, what kind of friends. Do you want to answer those questions?"

"I—" Theo's voice quavered. His cheeks flushed. "No. No, I don't."

Gabriel looked back at him. "Yeah. This is why I didn't ask."

The cathedral was modest, tucked a little out of the way. Almost hidden, to the extent a cathedral could be hidden, among the gleaming clothing stores and rustic brasseries. Only a few diners passed through the small square before it, on their way to their favourite haunts.

Gabriel took Theo's pack. "Break in, teleport somewhere, then come back to me. Oh, and don't go cheating. I might know."

He tapped his nose and winked, walking away. Theo gave a mock salute, then turned his attention back to the entrance. It had a tall rust-metal plate guarding it, enfolding the wooden double doors into the building proper. It was the only obvious sign the building was no longer a cathedral.

He strode right up to it, taking out the ring of keys given to him. He knew confidence was integral to the art of thievery and burglary, and now he knew it was integral to magic too. He eyed the metal on the lock. Black, nameless iron. Shame there was no brand name. Gabriel had told him there was only a small range of variation in modern keys, and companies would sell locksmiths identical blanks for a given lock.

He found a long lever key, as black as the lock, and inserted it.

It was the correct key.

Theo pushed through the doors, the hinges creaking into a dark, cavernous space. Moonlight streamed down from Gothic windows, illuminating stone columns to his left and reflecting off an enormous metallic structure to his right. He turned on the torch on his phone. A tower of bookcases extended along the entire nave of the cathedral, with a steel staircase and multiple floors. Past the top, he could just make out the vaulted ceiling bedecked with faded frescoes.

He clomped past the checkout, across commemorative slabs, taking in the books, the postcards, the teacups and the tote bags. There was another steel balcony tucked behind the arches to his left, and at the chancel, where the altar had been, was now a café. He stole a *stroopwafel*, tearing off the crinkly plastic packaging and tossing it in a pedal bin. He went behind the counter, found the cash box, and unlocked it. It was empty.

The embarrassment of asking Gabriel personal questions and being rebuffed weighed heavily on Theo. He didn't like the feeling. He decided to look for a book for his teacher. One he knew he didn't have. Yet, in his mind, Theo decided book-hunting would count as a demonstration of his skill. It didn't have to be an *apology*-apology. He hopped up the tower to peruse the English language section. He found *The Nonexistent Knight,* by Italo Calvino. Theo had never read it, but it looked like the kind of thing Gabe would enjoy. He plucked it off the shelf, tucked it inside his coat pocket, and pulled out a black marker to draw a sigil.

It was time to leave.

He decided to use the alchemical symbol of separation to mark the cathedral, no, the bookshop. It would be easy to remember it that way, given how disparate the parts of it were. This was the same symbol as the Scorpio sign, so he drew the little 'M' with a tail on one of the shelves. Then he focused. But he couldn't quite decide how to Regard this place. He and Gabriel had been to both bookshops and cathedrals. Yet, none of his previous destinations aligned with where he was now, and he couldn't think of anywhere as hybridised as this. It would be easiest to imagine it as a bookshop, but he couldn't scrub his perception of the cathedral. Those details felt integral to where he was now. His analysis was preventing synthesis.

Then, as he stood there all glum and gormless, the alarm went off. A high-pitched blare shocked his system and reverberated in the halls. Theo clapped his hands over his ears, but they couldn't keep it out. He could feel the noise throughout his body.

For a moment, he was reminded of home.

He hurried down the staircase, reaching the emergency exit, grabbing the push-bar. He stopped as he saw two police officers jogging towards the bookshop. They almost caught sight of him, but he threw himself backwards, slipping and slamming into the magazine shelves. Three Dutch models and an American movie star fell on his head. Slouched on the floor, he saw the twinkle of a security camera high above.

It was watching him. It was tying down his sympathy.

He scrambled up, scurrying back into the dark. He crashed into a shelf of teacups and fine china plates, sending an assortment of picture frames flying. The doors opened and he broke out into a sprint, blindly kicking a stack of self-help books left out in a long, low display. He reached a transept, which had been converted into the children's book section. He threw himself behind the display table.

A giant bunny plush stared at him from its nook.

The police were going to catch him. When the police caught him, he would be jailed. Worse, his photograph would be in the local newspaper, as some funny weirdo to laugh at. His magic would be gone. Then he'd need Gabriel's help again. If Gabriel wanted to help him. If he wanted to be near this embarrassment.

Theo's belly felt like it had been ripped out of him, as though something ate away at his insides. His shame was the only thing he could focus on, even as the police called out for the intruder. He cringed, hard, and stayed crouching in the dark for a long time. He did not know how long. When next he opened his eyes, he found himself outside in an alleyway, next to where he had asked Gabriel about his history.

Theo didn't know how he had teleported. He didn't know his shame had provided the vector.

He would never know this, because he would never want to think on it.

Theo had lost an hour in the hop, but his phone was quick to regain connection. He texted Gabe, who then shared his location. He had found a place for them to sleep underneath an overpass.

When Theo reached him, his teacher welcomed him with open arms.

"Faster than I would've believed. Well done. I hope there was no trouble?"

"No, none."

"Good. Very good. You've learned an important lesson. You need to be able to let go of details when they don't help you. I'm glad you've learned this."

Theo smiled and pulled out his pilfered book. "I got this for you."

"Oh, that's thoughtful. Thank you." Gabriel paused. "Theo, what I said before—"

"Forget it. You made a good point. My mistake."

Gabriel held the book. His expression wavered. "I haven't been to Curaçao in many years. The place where I grew up was a slave colony not so long ago. It had all the problems of places like this. Racism, discrimination, inequality. I don't need to tell you. Slavery had stopped many decades before I was born, but these things always leave their mark no matter how far back in time they start. They found oil off Venezuela, and Curaçao became a place to refine it. There was a lot of international interest. I worked in a Shell refinery for a few years when I was young, but it was difficult for locals. We weren't paid fairly. There were strikes, and later came some violence. I thought everything would become worse, and I wanted more of a life for myself. So, I left. I left behind everything and everyone I knew, and I went to America.

I didn't have money, but I had enough English and got to California. The people I met there told me I should go further west, or well, I guess we'd say east. Magic discovered me when I was in China. I thought about going back after that happened, but I didn't. I don't really know why. I'm sure my home is better these days, but I don't think I can call it home anymore."

He sighed and rubbed his rose tattoo. "To be honest, I have not looked back. I was raised there, but I've left it behind. It feels very selfish of me to say this, which is why I didn't want to talk about it before, but there's no reason not to tell you."

Theo didn't know what to say. He felt gratified for hearing it, at least. "Thanks, Gabe."

His teacher shrugged. "It's only fair, chief. If you can't be honest about life, you can't really live it."

In the days following Maastricht, Theo, now equipped with his keyring and a sense he could bail himself out of any situation, took over the role of thief. Contrary to Gabriel's staid and sober living arrangements, he started doing break-ins to fetch more luxurious meals, to find expensive booze and swanky hotel rooms. Hotels often keep rooms free in case of emergency bookings, and keycards were even easier to forge than keys. If anyone asked for his ID, he could transform his passport into something suitable.

Gabriel allowed him to indulge. He said it was good practice. Though, he didn't drink the liquor Theo stole and there was more than one occasion where he had to talk him out of robbing a bank. Anything so high-profile as a locked-room mystery would risk killing their magic.

Thievery taught Theo a few more tricks. When he teleported, he found it easiest to imagine the other side of a door was contiguous with his destination, allowing him to walk through to wherever he willed. Bathrooms became his preferred portals for that reason. You see a corporate bathroom; you could be just about anywhere. Polished marble and mirrors made for good hinges between dozens of locales, and they were kept clean to a pretty strict standard, unlike your standard dive bar lavatory. He felt quite confident he could have used the bathroom in Maastricht to escape, had he been prepared and known where it was.

In short order, Theo had obtained a competent grasp on teleportation and a standard of living he previously couldn't have envisioned for himself.

There was just one small problem. He was losing his mind with boredom.

Chapter Five

*But it is one thing to read
about dragons and another
to meet them.*

——*Ursula K. Le Guin, A
Wizard of Earthsea*

The pair had sequestered themselves away in a five-star room in Frankfurt. It had been a couple of weeks since Gabriel had last suggested anything for them to do. Theo decided a tour of five-star hotels was a worthy goal, but the fatigue of a long holiday had settled in. He sat on the bed, necking a bottle of wine and eating freshly stolen orange duck from the downstairs restaurant while Gabriel rifled through the bathroom for bars of soap and shower gel. Gabriel liked to collect the fancy toiletries.

"So..." Theo began. "Is this it?"

"What's that?" Gabriel called out. "Is there not enough duck?"

"No, no, I don't want more duck. I just..." He exhaled. "I don't know. Is this it? Do wizards just break into places? Don't they do anything else?"

Gabriel poked his head out, looking confused. "Like what?"

"I don't know." Theo dropped some duck onto the divan, staining it. He tried and failed to wipe it off. "This fine dining is fine and all, tautologically so. It's just... I don't know. I just thought I'd be applying this somehow. Not that I need a Sauron to slay, or a Narnia to govern, or what have you, but surely there's at least more magicians engaging in this penny-ante picaresque?"

"Magic doesn't mix with society, Theo. Remember?"

"Yes, I know, but are you really saying nobody is doing anything out there?"

Gabriel pursed his lips. "It's hard for me to say who's out there. None of us have a big network. I've heard about a couple of groups, but most of the solo magicians are studying magic by themselves. There's a lot about it we don't know, and it can help to work alone. Sometimes these people meet up with other magicians, share what they've learned, shed some light on things, and a new technique gets passed around. The thing with the keys was something I heard from a guy in Okinawa."

"See now, whatever else, that sounds more interesting than hotels."

"Yeah, but people who study too much magic alone turn out weird. I heard about a woman who was obsessed with going to the moon. It was the only thing she cared about. Only thing she'd ever talk about, or so they said. She even stole an old spacesuit from a museum."

"I'm guessing her project never got off the ground."

"Oh, she made it."

"What, really?"

"Well, she disappeared and never came back. Nobody knows what happened to her, or I never heard. I'd never met the person. Maybe she got there and died right away, or she got into space but missed the moon, or she's still stuck in a big travel lag, and she'll appear sometime in the future. Best as I can tell, nobody knows how magic treats space and other planets and so on. I doubt anyone does."

"Jesus. You think there's someone floating out there in the void?"

"Nah. If there was, NASA or someone would probably see. My thinking is she landed safely but her body is in the side of a crater or something."

"Why wouldn't she come back then?"

Gabriel shrugged. "The Overview Effect is my guess. When astronauts look back on the Earth from space, they say it changes how they see everything. Seeing the entire world, all at once, you can't think about it the same way anymore. I think that's what happened. She could connect the moon to the Earth before she really knew either of them. Once she knew them, this became impossible. They were too different. If she could have guessed how her own mind would change, then maybe we wouldn't have lost her."

Theo imagined dying alone on the moon. The colour fell from his face.

"I think you're right though," Gabriel said, apparently indifferent to Theo's reaction. "Maybe it's time you met some others. Apply your magic, as you say. There's only one group I know that don't do research. We can go looking for them tomorrow."

Gabriel reached behind the door and produced a bottle. "By the way, look at this. This one has the body scrub bits. I love when they have the body scrub bits."

"Great. It can scrub up this duck."

Initially, Theo imagined Gabriel bringing them to the real world of magic, with an ivory tower full of robed individuals uttering words of power. However, Gabriel didn't seem to know where they were headed. There were multiple possible destinations, and now he demanded speed, much more than before. Hopping between countries, their flights felt like drills, especially as Theo had to re-habituate himself to dirty hostels and cheap chain restaurants. Still, he refused to complain.

Theo had been to very few of the countries they visited. Eritrea, Madagascar, Guatemala, and several others. What's more, their destinations were often so remote they needed to be supplemented with a bus ticket or taxi ride, despite their magical means of transport. They never stayed in one country for long. They would arrive, briefly look around, and then move on within a couple of hours. The disillusionment brought about by public transit was, however, surpassed by that brought about by the sites themselves.

Theo soon realised what connected them: They were sites in need of humanitarian aid.

Refugee camps, slums, detention centres. Large prisons, remote villages under occupation. Places of famine, droughts, and floods. Places filled with forgotten people. Lands of privation, and people stripped bare. Theo thought himself street-hardened and capable, but there were many places far more dangerous than the streets of Berlin. When faced with desolation, his quips fell aside. He became quiet and withdrawn, unsure why Gabriel was bringing him on this tour. His discomfort grew until he could stand it no longer.

When the fear finally broke him, they were standing on a hill at the edge of a war zone.

A city was being bombed to pieces.

"What the bloody hell are we doing here, Gabe? Haven't these people got phones?"

Pale yellow shellfire lit the sky. A few seconds later, the boom reached them. They could see the eruption of concrete, a split cracking through the city. Theo didn't know what building had been there. He didn't know if it was a legitimate military target. He didn't know if it was empty. He couldn't bear to think about it. He couldn't bear to be there.

"Christ," he said. "This is awful. I can't handle this. I can't handle this, Gabe. I'm out. I'm sorry."

Gabriel snatched his hand and pulled him down to the ground. He sat with him.

"It's okay. You've said what I needed you to say, and you've seen what I needed you to see. I know this was tough, but we can move on now. The people we're looking for are in Los Angeles."

"Sorry, you mean—" Theo quailed at the sound of another boom. "Why *are* we here? Why are you bringing me to all these places? This is fucking dreadful."

Gabriel looked off into the breached horizon, as if searching for something he knew he would never find.

"To think they still sell books down there."

"What?"

"Nothing," he sighed. "Theo... What do you think magic is for?"

"I—what kind of question is that?"

"It's a simple one. Do you think it is so schoolboys with money can live in castles and become old men with long beards? Or is it so witches can entertain themselves with charms and potions? Do you think that's how a world of magic looks? Full of people speaking dead languages? Full of prophets saying everything's already doomed or saved, you need only wait for it to happen? That it's a world in which one special person can change everything?"

He took a breath. "The magic world. The human world. They're the same world. This one, with bombs and McDonald's. This is what it looks like. There is nothing above it. There is no grand order to it. If you want to use magic to improve the world, you'll use it in places like this."

There was another boom, and Gabriel looked back to Theo.

"I wanted you to see this. I wanted you to know it. Because if you don't want this, you can go back to the hotels, and I won't blame you. It's difficult to make a difference with magic. Hard work. But you can do it. I believe in you, now you know your limit."

Theo had been staring at the ground, afraid to look at everything around him. Yet, when he felt Gabriel's eyes on him, he felt all his teacher's expectations. More than that, he felt his own expectations. His own image of himself.

"Of course I want to use my magic, Gabe. That was the whole point of this jaunt. Did you think I was coming along for the exercise? For a light spot of trauma tourism? Honestly, if this is the next step, I don't know why we spent so much time in hotels. We could've jumped straight to the point."

"I needed time to train you. It's a dangerous world and you only have one life. Also, I was waiting to see if you'd get bored of comfort. I'm glad you did. I had some doubts."

"Gabe, you don't need to keep testing me or whatever it is you're doing."

"Yeah, I do. I'm your teacher."

"Yes, well, we've lost weeks with all this teleporting. I believe I only have one life."

Gabriel chuckled despite himself. "Okay. There's only so much I can do. I hope the enclave can teach you the rest of what you need. But Theo?"

"Yes?"

"Please remember, you can't fix everything."

Gabriel brought him to a homeless encampment on the outskirts of Los Angeles. A ragged tarpaulin flag had been set up in the middle of a parking lot, situating a throng of tents by an empty, sun-bleached supermarket. The tents were filled with people who would, that evening, be pushed outside city limits into the suburbs by cops. This was so the L.A. city council could pretend there were fewer unhoused people in their jurisdiction.

Sweat ran down Theo's neck. The day was baking hot. Plus, he had a keen sense of foreboding.

They went a couple blocks over to a dry grassy knoll, which overlooked the encampment. There, three people huddled around a blanket, on which lay several small packages and shopping bags. It looked to be some form of rag-tag distribution operation.

"Hello, lovely people," Gabriel said. "I brought my newcomer. Hope you can use him."

He strode forward while Theo was left behind, looking on like a child watching a parent meet their adult friends. There was a young woman with dyed-white hair and serious eyes. Gabriel shook her hand, clasping it with both of his own. A slight man with multiple piercings and a short mohawk hugged the big guy. The third person, an older woman with dreadlocks and a lined face, waved to Theo.

He waved back, wishing he'd stolen more alcohol when he had the chance.

The white-haired woman glanced in his direction and frowned.

"Is he going to say hi," she said with an Irish accent, "or just stand there?"

Gabriel smiled. "He's just shy. Come on over, Theo."

Theo trudged over. The pierced man and the dreadlocked woman came out to greet him, but the white-haired one crouched back down over the parcels.

"How do you do?" the pierced man asked, sticking his hand out. He spoke with a southern twang. "Name's Hanzo. I was the new guy before you, Mr. New Guy."

Theo shook his hand. "Hanzo. Pleasure. Like the ninja?"

Hanzo laughed and rubbed the back of his head. "Ain't heard that one in a while. Yeah, man, like Hattori Hanzo."

"Nice to meet you, Theo," the dreadlocked woman said. She had a strong German accent, and when she shook his hand, the smell of weed rolled off her like perfume. "I'm Maria."

"Ah. *Freut mich. Ich kann auch Deutsch wenn nötig.*"

She cocked an eyebrow at him. "Good to know, but German is not necessary. We mainly speak English, with other languages as required. Do you know any Urdu?"

"Uh," Theo said. "No, I don't."

"Tch, pity," Hanzo replied. "We could use an Urdu speaker. But hey, your German's welcome too, and you can always train it up with some Urdu. The more languages, the better, right, Mar?"

"Naturally," agreed Maria. "I've been learning Vietnamese."

Theo frowned, disappointed he couldn't flaunt his bilingualism. "Alright. So, what are we doing?"

"This," said the white-haired woman, as she sorted through the inventory on the ground.

"This is Sadhbh," Hanzo said. "She's friendly when she wants to be, I swear."

"Sorry," she said. "Don't want to lose count. Give me a minute."

Theo first spotted an orange bottle of pills and, for a fraction of a second believed it was preparations for drug dealing, until he noticed her extract two yoghurt drinks and some lentils from one of the shopping bags, wrapping them up along with the pills.

"Retail duty?" he asked, then caught himself. "No, of course not. Pardon me. I guess we'll be taking a trip somewhere?"

Sadhbh shot him a look, then turned to Gabriel. "Did you tell him what we do?"

"Thought it best to hear from you. I did the tour, though."

"You love to waste time," she muttered. She picked up a pen and marked something on a notepad to the side. Then she turned to Theo. "Well, new fella, you've been taught that only outcasts can do magic, right?"

Theo was taken aback. "Uh, sure."

"You know that having connections prevents magic?"

"Yes."

"Good. Here's the problem. When you're on the margins, you need to band together with others to survive. But, if you do that, you'll create a sympathetic network, potentially with many solid connections. This creates a problem for magic. So, there are clusters of people who need magic and might have it if it weren't for their number. Many of them, as it happens. The homeless encampment over there's an example.

"What we do is deliver things to those that need them. Food, medicine, messages, valuables if they barter things. Sometimes we do manual labour. Patch a roof, clear a road, and replace some wiring. Can't do much of that, though. Have to be inconspicuous. When we make drop-offs, we make them look like luck. Try not to get personally involved. Too much notice and our own magic goes away. We can't ever give enough to make a recognisable difference, but the upside is we stop some folks from starving to death or dying of TB. That's the job, and that's what you're helping with. Move from crisis to crisis, keep to the fringes, and minimise harm. Got it?"

Theo didn't fully take in the staccato chatter from Sadhbh, though her tone made his hackles rise all the same. Nevertheless, he stayed quiet. He didn't want to cause a scene in front of Gabriel.

Hanzo groaned. Catching Theo's eye, he mimed shooting himself with a pistol. "It ain't half so bad as she makes out. We also like to have a little fun too. You should know you won't find another gathering of magicians like this. We can swap a lot of stories and techniques. Maria can tell you plenty about spirits, and I like to think I'm an okay cook."

"Spirits?" Theo looked at his teacher. "Spirits exist?"

"Oh, yes. They're rare. Maria can teach you more about them than me."

Maria folded her arms. "I don't think that's true."

"Yes, it is," Gabriel replied.

"This recruitment vibe is weird," Theo said, half-joking. "Feels like I'm being advertised to by the tooth fairy. Some kind of mutually-aiding Santa-Claus-collective."

"Gabe, do we have to keep this guy?" Sadhbh rolled her eyes.

Gabriel shrugged. "He has talent. He needs friends. You can smooth each other out, no?"

"Wait," Theo said, "You're leaving? I thought you were sticking around?"

"I train new magicians, chief. You're no longer one."

The words stung Theo. He had been under the assumption that his relationship with Gabriel was a personal one. It hadn't occurred to him that he might be just the next student in line, that where he thought there was friendship had been only a kind of professional courtesy.

Gabriel rested a hand on Theo's shoulder. "You okay? You can go your own way if this doesn't fit. You wouldn't be the first, you know."

Theo waved him away, plastering a big smile across his mug. "Oh I know. You don't need to tell me. I think I've gotten everything I can from you anyhow. You get going big guy, and I'll get settled."

"I'm usually in Shenzhen if you need me. You still have my number, too."

"Yeah, yeah. *Ciao*, *sayonara*, and see you later."

Gabriel smiled, "*Te aworo*, Theo."

The big man bid his goodbyes to the others. Then he sauntered away, hands in pockets, disappearing down into the urban warren below where he was swallowed up by the bustle of other bodies.

"Always good to get a visit from Gabriel," Hanzo said.

"Yes," Maria agreed. "Pity he can't spend time with us."

Theo snagged a bottle of water and took a healthy swig from it. "Alrighty then. What's on the docket for today, Amnesty Supernatural?"

Hanzo winced. "Dude, don't take things that are going out. We keep an inventory."

"Really? It's just water."

Sadhbh snatched the water from his grip. She wiped the top with her sleeve and placed it back where it belonged.

"Listen. We don't need comedians. We need workers. Can you work?"

"Uh, yeah. Of course."

"Then follow me."

Chapter Six

'Well, well! Who'd have
thought it!' exclaimed
Charlemagne. 'And how do
you do your job, then, if you
don't exist?'

'By will power,' said Ag-
ilulf, 'and faith in our holy
cause.'

—Italo Calvino, The
Nonexistent Knight

Theo's introduction to the work was a gentle one, which, in
many ways, set him up for failure. The first week consisted
merely of secreting food and water away in the corners of various tent
cities, but this was only a small project. If Gabriel hadn't given him his
earlier tour, Theo might not have been able to keep up with the pace
of the real work.

Sadhbh assigned him the role of supplier, alongside Hanzo. They both carried keyrings and blank keycards for burglary, but really their main responsibility was developing and remembering routes to supplies, and taking advantage of delays between time zones to enter them when nobody would be around. The system of sigils he had developed with Gabriel came into full effect here. Hanzo, for his part, carried around several sheets of emoji stickers that he could place wherever he needed.

As a supplier, Theo was constantly on the move. If he wasn't actively developing routes to supplies, then he was being deployed to fetch them. If children in Sierra Leone needed clothing, Sadhbh would send him to the Atacama Desert in Chile. It was the world's dumping ground for fast fashion. He'd pick through the dusty dunes of Uniqlo loungewear and tech pants from Urban Outfitters to find suitable garments. If families in Afghanistan couldn't get the medicine they needed thanks to trade embargoes, then he'd be sent to break into the distribution centres of Pfizer or Johnson & Johnson. He'd carry a small crate or two back to Kabul, whatever he figured wouldn't be missed. If refugees in Libyan detention camps needed phones or chargers to contact their relatives, then he'd be off to raid a consumer electronics shop in France. He'd give a few families the means to survive the Mediterranean. He would rarely make the deliveries himself, however. Maria would typically be the one to drop off the goods, while he rested and Sadhbh planned the next steps.

Each time they arrived somewhere new, one of the central trio would receive a notification from their contacts, the news, or non-magical aid agencies, informing them about a new crisis somewhere else and what might be needed. Sadhbh would calculate what they had and how to move the resources around most efficiently. She would plan weeks of travel at a time, as the days lost in transit ensured the enclave's phones were always alive. There were always new messages pending.

There was a drought. There was a flash flood. An earthquake. Another.

Hunger. Hunger. War and slaughter.

So on, and so forth.

There was too much happening for them to visit all the places in need. Even restricting it only to the locations of highest priority, there was too much, but Sadhbh mixed less urgent crises in with the more urgent ones. This was done to keep the enclave safe, and, Theo suspected, to keep them mentally sound.

Each stop offered him only the merest glimpse of these places. He knew in every location he failed to comprehend some part of the problem, that he grasped only a sliver of the full picture. He barely touched these places, barely saw the people he helped, and the demanding nature of the job got to him. He felt out of his depth, intimidated by his newfound peers and the severity of the situations they faced and knew so much better. Consequently, he remained on the fringes of the group, drinking ever more pilfered liquor.

It was a cold evening in the mountains of Nagorno-Karabakh, and Theo wasn't spending it with the enclave. While the others sat around a fold-out table in their overcoats, exchanging cards in a game of rummy, Theo departed. He said he was too tired. He took his guitar and a bottle of gin and found a fallen pine tree, against which he sat and strummed.

From here, the land of Nagorno-Karabakh seemed to him like a blanket. A thick one, of green and grey, which rumpled up into hills and rocky ravines or spread out in alpine meadows, with medieval monasteries tucked away in its folds like cookie crumbs. There was little mist that night, though there had been much more in the month prior. The magicians had been secreting away caches of money and supplies for Armenians, but this had come to an end. They had given all they could and the Azerbaijani army had begun to move in. The Armenians were leaving in droves. Only a fraction of a fraction of their hundreds of thousands had received their aid. Many of them were burning down their houses as they left, to deny anything to the army.

Theo knocked back a mouthful of gin and continued to strum. It was an awkward, halting tune. His fingers felt clumsy as he moved them across the strings, as if feeling them for the first time. The place felt like it was taking something from him, but he didn't know what.

"I reckon I know what you're playing."

Theo jumped. Hanzo had sneaked up on him and grinned at catching him out. His piercings glinted like sparks in the mountains' sunset.

"It's the song for this place, right? 'Nagorno-Karabakh?' Einstürzende Neubauten?"

"A cover of a cover," Theo muttered. "I don't have the proper guitar for it. Surprised you can recognise it, to be honest."

"I know my music. Anyhow, it's not the first time I've been here. We're named for this place you know. Or places like it, at any rate. A bunch of people, kept separate, trying to get by in the middle of something much bigger than themselves—that's an enclave."

"You've got to be surrounded by a singular piece of foreign territory for it to be an enclave. Otherwise, it's just an exclave."

"That's nice. I'll make that word of the day. Now will you move over?"

Theo sidled over, and the punk plonked down beside him. "You know, those Einstürzende guys never gave a hoot about having the right instruments. They dug up scrap metal and banged on it until it sounded right. I might could do the same on this here stump."

"Don't you want to play cards?"

"Rummy's not my game, it's Sadhbh's." Hanzo walked up to the top of the tree. He broke off a long, desiccated twig, and knelt beside Theo. "Now, let her rip."

Theo played, while Hanzo banged on the tree, using his fist, his palm, and the twig. He kept a good rhythm, despite his instruments. They played for a few minutes, until Theo played a bum note and lost his place.

"Fuck's sake" he swore. "Sorry. I'll do it properly."

"Don't worry, we're just jamming."

"I said I'll do it properly."

Theo struggled on, but now the music sounded lonely to his ears. He couldn't bring himself to sing, only to mouth the words under his breath. He stopped once more, sighing.

"How do you guys do it?" he asked. "Day in, day out, without seeing anyone?"

"How do you mean? You're not looking for thank-yous, I take it?"

"No, no, of course not. It's just... I never knew about all these places we visit. The Sahel, Myanmar... I never knew what was happening in them. Some, sure, but there's so many. And I don't know how you keep the people distinct. I don't know how you can know anything about the people you're helping."

"Huh. Yeah. Good question. I guess we just take the broad view. Look at the stats, see what's what. It's the only way we got to keep it all in perspective, and that's what we got to do. Anywho, how much you got to know about a person before you decide to care about them?"

"Yes, but how can you ever decide to move on?"

The magician propped himself up on the log by his elbows, and exhaled in a long, drawn-out breath. "Because we're doing triage man. That's all this ever is. It's nothing glamorous. I mean, you're likely right. Anything we could do will be blown out the water by people sticking in place and doing real social change. Real reform. Might be the right thing for us to do is to accelerate that. Give up on all this and kidnap a dictator or a tech mogul, sabotage a few oil refineries, hell, just syphon a few billion off Wall Street and go into microfinancing. Expend all our magic in one big blow-out and do something that really shakes things up. I've thought about it. We've all thought about it. Maybe it'd be more effective, but—"

"But the vulnerable will suffer the backlash," Sadhbh finished. She and Maria walked over to the two men. They sat down beside them. "If a boat is rocked, those on the edge fall off."

"Hey Sadhbh," Hanzo waved the twig at them. "Who won that round?"

"I did," Maria said.

"Congrats. Hope y'all don't mind us sneaking away. We felt like playing some music."

Sadhbh gave a feeble shake of her head. "I don't mind."

Maria pulled out a modified Game Boy. "I actually wanted to join the music."

"What are you doing with that old thing?" Theo asked.

"Is it so old?" She examined it in bemusement. "It has a long battery life, and I can make it play music."

She turned on the purple box. It dinged to life, and in a couple of minutes Maria had it playing a few spare, steady, glassy sequences. Despite the old sound card, there was an ethereal quality to the noise. Hanzo banged on the tree once more, and Theo found himself plucking the strings again. For a moment, there was music. Not quite the same as the song, but similar enough. For a moment, there was something like peace, until they smelled smoke on the wind, and Sadhbh stood up to see a dark plume rising from the foot of the mountain.

"A house?" she asked. "So close to camp? How did we miss it?"

The music stopped again, save for the chimes of Maria's makeshift synth.

"You should sit down," she said.

"They must not have been on the maps." Sadhbh paced to the overlook's edge. "And I never saw them. They're burning down their home, and I never saw them. We have to do something."

"We have no more supplies to give them. There's nothing we can do."

"They'll need something. They can use something. We have food. Water."

Maria snatched Sadhbh's arm and pulled her down. "If they've already set fire to the house, then they are already moving. If they are moving, then you risk being seen. If you're seen, then all the good we have done here will belong to you. Do you understand? They will think about you."

Sadhbh yanked her arm away. "If I'd been doing my job right then this wouldn't be an issue. It's my mistake. I need to fix it."

"You plan the deliveries, but there's a reason you don't do them. You're close to burning out."

"But I—"

"Sadhbh, you're close to dissolving. You need to take care of yourself. There are other places that need us. They need us right now."

With that, she appeared to regain focus. "Right," she said, nodding. "You're right."

She pulled her hands down across her face, pressing them against her lips, as if trying to wipe the exhaustion from her mind. She kicked the dirt before her. The cloud of dust drifted out to the horizon, joining the smoke.

There was an awkward pause, and then she shot up once more.

"I'll just see if there's anyone else I missed," she said. "Won't be long. I won't help unless I see someone staying. Promise."

She headed down the mountain at a brisk pace.

"Sadhbh!" Maria called out, but the white-haired woman didn't look back. Maria got up to follow her, leaving Hanzo and Theo behind. "Please excuse me Theo, but I won't be able to play music with you."

They sat in silence for a little while. It seemed like there was no point in music anymore.

"It's getting dark," Theo said. He stood up and dusted himself down. "Sadhbh will want the camp packed when she returns. There's my guitar there if you want. There's gin too. Have at it."

"Nah, that's alright. I'll join you. You'll need a hand packing up."

"No," Theo said. "I think I'd like to be alone, if that's okay."

Hanzo's shoulders fell, but he nodded. "Sure. I get it."

Some time after "Nagorny-Karabach," the enclave visited Galicia for a reprieve. Millions of plastic pellets had spilled off a shipping container, swamping the northwest coast of Spain. Sadhbh and Maria joined the clean-up crews, while Theo and Hanzo sourced chemical retardants for the wildfires likely to spring up in summer, developing routes in case of emergency. Once Theo had developed his route, he found himself alone for a couple of days in the city of A Coruña. This was where he made his first significant mistake.

He decided to indulge himself in the local cuisine.

He visited several restaurants, where he ate heavily, as though he were merely a traveller stopping by. He gorged himself on bowls of *caldo Gallego*, heapings of *navajas*, *gambas ajillo*, and *pimientos de Padrón*, and the dry, sweet *tortas de Santiago*, all bought using money stolen from wealthy tourists.

When Sadhbh returned from the shore, she found him at a restaurant, paying the bills.

"Theo? What are you doing here?"

"Hello to you too, Sadhbh. You're as polite as ever. You want wine?"

"No, I don't. You shouldn't be eating this."

"What? Why not? This is one of the cheaper places around. I checked. Cross my heart on that one."

"It's not the price. You need to avoid sensory diversions. Especially local cuisine. You'll get stuck."

"What are you talking about?"

"Trapped by a place. The details will overload your magic. Too specific. Go for processed foods and generic staples. Bread, salad, canned tuna. Non-local fare. If it's shipped internationally, it's fine."

"I ate rather well when I was with Gabe. It wasn't a problem then."

"Did you eat German food when you were in Germany? Or did you get take-out?"

"Mostly take-out. It was nicer. But what does it matter? I can handle it."

"I'm serious. No more of it."

Theo laughed, "Okay mum, no more garlicky shellfish."

Theo didn't think there was much to Sadhbh's comments, but when the time came to move to the next destination in South Sudan, he found the tastes and smells of Galicia grounded him. He couldn't Regard. He couldn't ignore the particularities of Galicia because here and only here did they have their particular cuisine, which was still fresh on his lips, warm in his belly, and firmly embedded in his memory.

It was the cathedral in Maastricht, once again.

Only this time, the others didn't wait around. They didn't come back.

Theo thought about giving up then. The work was overwhelming him. It wasn't that any particular task was too demanding, more that it was to be worked on endlessly. It was the dreariness of it. The quotidian nature of magical work, now made all the duller and harder without creature comforts.

As he began to hitchhike along the coastline, he saw an end where he left and drifted all desultory as before, back to living bohemian, though now with the certainty of finding room and board every night. Perhaps he'd be bored again, but maybe boredom was the better feeling. At least you can own your own boredom. You can do something about it. You can scratch the itch. Indulge it. Gratify it. Pacify it.

You can't scratch away a feeling of impotence.

Yet, he knew he couldn't leave. If he left, Gabriel would find out.

It was the fear that Sadhbh had spoken to Gabriel that spurred Theo on. It was shame and the fear of shame that made him rinse his mouth out with frozen pizzas, and find a route to Sudan.

When he rejoined the enclave, they were still there, on a dusty, stone-strewn hill with orange shafts of sunlight beaming down. They were packing trauma kits for covert delivery. Upon his return, Sadhbh brought him to one side before he could greet the others.

"Because of your absence, our scheduling has been knocked back a fortnight. I don't know what Gabriel was doing with you, but we are *not* here to babysit you. We don't have time. Wise up or fuck off."

Then she moved past him. She had no further interest in him.

It didn't help that of the four of them, the fastest was Sadhbh. He stared at her as she walked away, and felt his resentment grow. Sadhbh, who never partook in any local dishes, who drove the group ever onward, who was ever on the lookout for more folk to help. She was like a gargoyle squatting on the side of a church. He could smell the sanctimony off her.

Over the following days, his resentment grew and developed, feeding on the disquiet he had felt before. It disturbed him how the other magicians would sacrifice days or weeks to journeys at Sadhbh's behest. How whole chunks of life would be fed to the cause, like a mangy dog being thrown scraps.

He remembered how warmly Gabriel greeted her.

Theo wasn't going to leave. He needed to be better than Sadhbh.

He would have to prove this, of course.

Chapter Seven

One has to be wounded in
order to become a healer.

—Marie-Louise von Franz,
The Problem of the Puer
Aeternus

One night, Theo and Hanzo shared a campfire in North Korea. Out of everyone, he liked Hanzo the best, and hoped the punk rocker felt the same way. Given that Hanzo had recently lapsed back into smoking and shared his cigarettes with Theo, Theo considered their friendship vindicated.

"So..." Theo started as his friend pulled a roast chicken off a spit. "How do you lot manage to move faster than me?"

He tugged at his sleeves, conspicuously attempting to appear casual.

"Awh, don't be worried about that. There's no tricks to it. Comes with time."

"Who said I'm worried? I'm not worried. What I am, if anything, is impatient."

"Alright. Whatever you say. Either way, it comes with time."

"It would also save me some grief from Sadhbh."

"Ah," Hanzo started cutting into the chicken. "So that's your problem. Well, you know what she's like, but she'll ease up. She was hard on me for the first half-year or thereabouts. Don't let her age fool you. She's been doing this for a long time. I think coming on thirty years now."

"Thirty years?" Theo frowned. "She doesn't look so old."

"Oh yeah, but you don't age when you hop. I meant thirty years of real-time. If you go by the calendar, she's got to be fifty or sixty years old. I don't know her age in personal-time. I'd guess she's been doing this for five or six years. Like I said, though, don't take it personally. You get real removed from the world the more you do magic. You miss a lot of life. But hey, it does make you quicker."

Hanzo began parcelling the meat out into small tortillas. "I miss music, myself. Memphis was putting out good stuff back when I lived there. But that's something a little too geographic, so I don't listen to it so much these days. Not just the instruments but the scene, too. You'd know. You're from Berlin."

"Music's a rather big thing to sacrifice for a little charity."

"Charity?" Hanzo tilted his head. "Is that what you think this is? I guess you could call it that, but we save people. It's meaningful work. Most folks never get the chance to do something meaningful. It's a kind of escape if you ask me."

"Escape? We're constantly working on such depressing things. How is this an escape?"

Hanzo nodded in thought. He knew he hadn't said it quite right. He passed Theo a paper plate with a tortilla, along with some lettuce and red onion, and a squeezy mayonnaise bottle. "What I mean is... Out in the world, right, people get wrapped up in things they know on some level are fake. They get told to do work that doesn't need to be done. They get told they need things they don't want, or to fear things that aren't scary. They get separated from reality. They know the world they're in doesn't add up. And they know something is wrong, but they can't articulate it to themselves. And that's scary. Reality gets scary, because it's so complicated. So folks look for quick comfort or easy answers. It's not their fault, but that only brings them deeper into the labyrinth, and then they start to really go cuckoo bananas. Now, I'm not saying magic is the ticket out of all this. Magic is making up connections between things. If that's all we did, I reckon we'd be adding to the problem. But I think the work we do with it is real work. I see how it fits into things. It matters, and I think that brings us a little closer. It's not an escape into reality, but it's an escape towards reality."

Theo dressed his wrap, and chewed on it slowly. He thought about mentioning the problems he was having, his doubts, but words failed him. It felt like another wrong moment, in a sea of false opportunities. He couldn't think of a way to phrase it that would guarantee Hanzo would still like him.

"Well, that was all very Gnostic of you," he said.

"Hah. That brings me onto something I've been wondering about you. You don't seem like you come from money, but some of the things you come out with sound college-educated. What's your deal?"

Theo was taken aback by the question. He hid his surprise by attending to the wrap.

"What's there to say? I like to read."

Hanzo didn't give a reply. He waited for Theo to continue.

Theo blew a raspberry and said, "I don't know. I've always been a swot. Kept the boredom at bay at school. I'd read textbooks in my own time. If the mood struck me, I'd read far ahead of everyone else, even reading through the night or reading supplemental materials. There are times when I become very passionate about things. The habit never really left me."

"Hey man, that's a good way to be."

"Yes, well, my teachers didn't appreciate it. They were so slow, and so were all the others in my classes. I'd have a textbook read all the way through before they passed the halfway mark. I'd just have to sit there and let them drone on and on, or else begin reading something else only to be reprimanded for not paying attention. It was maddening. I'd get so frustrated with them that I'd start saying the answers out loud to try and speed things up, which obviously pissed everyone off. This wasn't half so bad as when the teachers were objectively incorrect. I'd have to correct them, and they would get into a proper furore about my 'being disruptive' or whatever it was. They'd do the usual—get me to stay behind after school, make phone calls with my parents, threaten me with suspension. The principal, of course, did not get the principle issue, which was that I was fucking bored."

Theo paused, deciding what he wanted to admit. He omitted the worst of his pains, and adjusted the remainder. "Their remedy was to stick me in a separate classroom by myself, which worsened the situation because it was even duller and… Well. The long and short of it is I was kicked out before I ever did my A-levels."

"A-levels… those are your high school exams, right? That's rough, dude. Sorry to—"

"Psh. It was liberating. I wasn't stuck in that place, wasting my time. I could read what I wanted or practise my music. Didn't have any obligations holding me back. Hanzo, my friend, I was unshackled."

"Sure, but getting kicked out must've hurt."

Theo fell silent, and stared up at the night sky. A sickle moon hung over them.

"I remember lying in a field the week I was expelled. It was a night just like tonight. I was looking up at the stars. They shone as brightly then as they do now. Which is strange. We're so much farther from built-up areas here."

"You needed to get away from it all, I'm guessing?"

"Truthfully, I was in a brilliant mood. I remember thinking how amazing it was to see all these stars simultaneously. How phenomenal it was that my consciousness could fit the entire universe inside of it. I mean that both literally and metaphorically. All those stars were in me, in my mind, just as my body is composed of elements made in them. What could something as small as school mean to me when I was one with the cosmos? In a way, I was invulnerable."

"I don't agree, but I can respect it." Hanzo chuckled. "Either way, sounds like you were trippin'." He stared up at the stars with Theo.

"You know, that makes me think, maybe I do have a trick for you after all."

"Oh really? What?"

"Psychedelics."

"Oh, now that's interesting. Yes, please. How do they help? Which kind is best?"

"You're real torn up about your speed, ain't you?" Hanzo laughed. "Well, if you want the technical answer, I can give it. See, psychedelics up the entropy of the brain. Entropy's another word for randomness, right, chaos? So, more random connections get made between neurons and likewise between concepts. If you think of your brain as an ice cube, psychedelics heat it up. They get the water flowing. It's useful for seeing things fresh. It's why they can be useful for therapy. Sometimes, the brain gets frozen into bad shapes and needs loosening up. That's how you get thousands of years' worth of mystical traditions founded on ritualistic tripping, you know? So yeah, psychedelics can accelerate you. As for what's best: peyote, ayahuasca, or whatever floats your boat. Though, you probably want a low dose if you want to keep moving."

"What about actual speed? Amphetamines, I mean. Or other drugs?"

"If you're fixin' to use them, go right ahead, but there's no special benefit so far as I know. You want psychedelics. Maybe an entactogen could help too, come to think of it. MDMA, that kind of thing. The main thing is you're breaking down your walls. Letting yourself be open to things you aren't open to normally."

"Do you know a lot about this?"

Hanzo licked his teeth. "Oh man, I could get way more technical on the cognitive science side. There's lots of philosophy of mind stuff that's pretty off-the-grid but useful for us. Similarity's actually a real dilly of a pickle for philosophers. One theory I like though is that it's about finding a structural representation that efficiently maps two domains. Seeing which parts of one structure mirror the parts of another. You only need a weak isomorphism, but if you use the same mappings as other people, that strengthens it. Intersubjective alignment. That gets your neurons firing in resonance. That's what makes the magic happen."

Theo blinked. Hanzo gave him a meat-filled grin.

"I'm an autodidact, too, man. Actually, that's another thing that can help you out. Find some discipline that helps you structure your magic. Helps with the process. The old traditions have sigils and symbols, and they got their place, but you don't have to do that. I got my cognitive science, but Maria studies physical geography and tech and Sadhbh's into history. What were you doing before you got into this?"

"I was a musician." Theo glanced away.

"Oh, right, yeah. Of course." Hanzo scratched his head. "Okey-doke, well, listening to music doesn't work for me, but maybe you can read up on world music or something. Figure out how things influenced each other. Berlin's got its techno roots in Detroit, after all, right? And that French guy, Debussy, he was influenced by gamelan? That's from Indonesia, if I recall rightly."

Theo wasn't sure, but he said, "Yes, I've heard that's correct."

"There you go. Now you've got links to help you out."

They finished the rest of their meal and began to clean up.

"Honestly though, Theo, I don't think you should be stressing too much. The real reason we're faster is because we've done it longer. If you do your job long enough, the world will lose its grip on you. It's sad, really. After a while, all this travelling becomes a run through a list of names. Places stop feeling like places. You don't want to rush to that."

"Thanks, Hanzo. I appreciate it."

"No worries, man."

"Hey, Hanzo?"

"Lemme guess. Another smoke?"

"Yes, please."

Chapter Eight

*Estragon: We always find
something, eh Didi, to give
us the impression we exist?*

*Vladimir: Yes, yes, we're
magicians.*

*——Samuel   Beckett,
Waiting for Godot*

Theo started to settle into the group. He became more open
and, to the mildest degree, found himself somewhat at home.
He even played his old guitar a bit, and Sadhbh didn't protest too
strenuously. There were nights he forgot he wanted to be alone, not
merely because weed or something harder obscured the desire. There
were nights being part of a group felt... normal.

Another night, he arrived on a grassy knoll outside Dublin, Georgia
to drop off a crate of methadone. He was markedly late, having worked
so hard to avoid landing in the country of Georgia or the capital of
Ireland that he had instead been waylaid by Dublin, California, and

feared more acrimony from Sadhbh. He hurried through verdant walls of shortleaf pine to find the campsite, but once he made his way through the thicket, instead of Sadhbh, he found Maria and Hanzo arguing over a plastic box of USB sticks.

Maria was shielding the box with her body.

"Let me have them," she said. "The spirits aren't dangerous. They're very small."

"Awh, c'mon, Mar, we've talked about this. You can't bring your stolen junk back to camp. You draw too much heat."

"We can teleport."

"Agh, that's not—"

"What's with the sticks?" Theo asked.

Maria swivelled around, her dreadlocks swishing like beaded curtains. "Hello, Theo. Good to see you. I have found several vessels for schizograms, which I intend to study. Perhaps you would join me?"

"Hey, hey," Hanzo put an arm in front of her. "Don't use Theo as an out. We're not having another San Francisco. Theo, man, get this: we were doing an aid drop for the unhoused folks out there, standard stuff like you'd done before when Mar here decides to 'port into Facebook's HQ and go spirit-hunting on their servers. She causes a massive outage, trips an alarm and gets locked inside a server room. Now the 5-0 are on the way, so yours truly has to go inside and set off the damn fire alarm to open the automatic locks. Isn't that right, Mar?"

"That happened only one time."

"Yeah, well, if it's not crap like that, it's you neglecting inventory."

"It's *your* turn to do inventory."

As they argued, Theo stepped forward and plucked a stick from Maria's box. It looked cheap. Plain, silver, metallic. There was nothing to indicate any particular significance.

"Sadhbh said Theo needed more education," Maria said. "This is an opportunity."

Hanzo ran his hand through his mohawk. He sighed. "Fine. Screw it. Knock yourselves out."

Once he had left, Theo and Maria crouched around the box, picking through sticks. Theo had no idea what he was looking for, so he studied Maria as she held one in her hand, concentrating. Her focus was so intense that it seemed she forgot Theo was there, prompting him to speak.

"Are you gonna tell me about these spirits?"

"Spirits are what happens when sympathy gets a life of its own," she replied, placing the stick to one side and fetching another. "Sympathy is a network of connections, yes? Well, some networks are like the circulatory system. There's only one part, the heart, which provides all the movement and all the connections. This is you when you Regard. Then there are other networks, like the internet, where all the parts talk with each other independently. They all provide movement, and the network takes on a kind of life. This is what spirits are. They are what happens when beliefs reinforce themselves. They are rare. Hard to find, even for us, and we don't fully understand them. One thing we know is that many spirits prefer certain types of houses. These sticks are houses for schizograms. The name means 'split-writing' or 'split-recording.' Schizograms have been known about for a long time, so they have a Greek name."

"What do they do?"

"They're created when people view objects in contradictory ways. USB sticks are common. People think they need to be inserted one way; many think the other way, so you have contradictions. This makes a little daemon who prevents insertion either way. To defeat a schizogram, one must go through all the ways it can be. For a USB stick, you rotate it and try inserting it three times. Some seatbelts are also like this, with a schizogram inside them. You might also find doors that need to be pushed and pulled before they can be opened."

Theo watched as Maria picked up another stick. Her concentration took on new significance. It became part of a ritual to consult another world, to summon intelligences that were not human. Attention, he realised, is the art of seeing what is there.

"Are there other spirits?" he asked, with his voice low.

"There are more modern ones. When I broke into Facebook, I was looking for a marshmind, which is much bigger. They're created when people Regard internet algorithms as real things. They live on servers and eat attention. This is why people will watch three-hour videos on YouTube about something they've never heard of, but they cannot watch a movie, even if the movie is very good. I thought Facebook servers would have a big one, so I killed it by changing their IP protocols."

She smiled at her recollection, but her smile flickered. "There were also many spiderbrains there, which I didn't kill. They come when others online assume you have an opinion you don't because your profile picture makes you look like seven others they know who do. They make people irrationally angry, so those opinions are never corrected, and the spirit thrives. And there are the kirkteeth, which exist in airports, waiting rooms, supermarkets, and clothing stores. These are places where people get very bored, all made to feel similar to each other. A kirktooth is difficult to deal with. They drain the energy out of people and can do a lot of harm. They are related to even nastier spirits."

"How do you know one is there? Can you communicate with them?"

She shrugged. "You listen closely when you Regard objects. You'll sometimes hear them talk to you. It's the same belief when you are duplicating objects, only with more focus."

"You seem rather good at focusing, if I may say so."

"I had to learn it. I've been to lots of places I shouldn't have gone, places that were hard to leave. As I learned magic, I liked to go caving. I'd use magic to step in, and then walk around. I thought that since magic was real, there must be magical places. I thought these would be secret places, where nobody had ever been, hidden in the Earth. Anyway, the first time, I went to Krubera Cave. It was the deepest we knew of at the time, so I thought there would be lots of room. This wasn't true at all. Caves are mostly just cracks in the ground. I wasn't prepared for how small they are. How close they press, like they want to squeeze the air out of you. Photographs of caves are only of places where light can shine, and there's not many. The first time I went to a cave, my leg got stuck in a crack. I had to wait for it to go numb before I could imagine I was somewhere else, and teleport. These days, they say Krubera is the most dangerous cave in the world, but I didn't know that at the time. My next journeys went much better though, for the most part."

Theo's eyebrows raised. "You went back underground?"

"Yes. I learned what it was like to be stuck, so I wasn't worried."

"If you're such an expert explorer, how'd you get locked in a server room?"

Her mouth twisted into a smile. "The alarm was loud. It distracted me."

Theo remembered his burglary in Maastricht. "Oh. I know that feeling."

"If it happens to you again, my advice is to sit with the feeling. If you are afraid, then let yourself be afraid, and watch how the fear changes your thoughts. Do not act on the fear. You must understand your situation if you want to leave it."

"I guess that's why Hanzo had to rescue you."

"The alarm was very loud."

Theo drew his knees up to his chest. He reflected on how little magical education he'd really had. How confident he had been after damaging a single golden fry in China. There were depths to it he had never considered and which Gabriel had never brought up. The eating, the ageing, the whole spirit world. Yet, he thought, the critical point remained apparent. Magic was nothing more than a metaphysical con job. It was all about belief. Nothing more.

"This is a lot of time to spend on this. I can't imagine Sadhbh is happy about you moonlighting as a paranormal investigator. It's not part of the supply run job, is it?"

"No. Not really. It's a less dangerous way for me to explore."

"Would it be okay if I looked for one, too?"

"Yes. I would like it if you did."

They sat together for half an hour as they sorted through the sticks. As he Regarded his, Theo tried to imagine what a USB spirit would sound like. It could sound like a little goblin and say funny insults in a regional accent. He'd like that. Or perhaps because it was in an electronic device, it'd speak with the clipped voice of a computer, with Linux commands or something.

They sat there for a long while, passing through most of the sticks without incident when Theo, holding a matte red one, heard a voice.

VERSO RSOVE RECTO CTORE

"What?" he whispered, unsure if he was imagining it.

LEFT FTLE RIGHT GHTRI

"Oh my god. Maria. I've found one."

"Good. Stay calm. Listen to it. Then you can ask it questions."

At that moment, Sadhbh burst out of the thicket, arms laden with supplies. Theo cringed when he saw her and lost his connection to the schizogram.

Sadhbh dropped down her inventory and called out to the camp. "Alright, everyone, I had a delayed hop, so we need to finish these drop-offs sharpish. Next stop is Rio. Oi Theo, have you not unpacked the methadone yet? Should have been done as soon as you arrived. Get to it."

"Do you mind?" Theo asked. "I'm communing with spirits."

"Yeah, I do mind." Sadhbh rummaged around in their bags. "Got notice of some unrest in Brazil. Major protests. Maybe riots. We need to get on top of them. Keep your lip to yourself and try not to fuck up on this hop. And hurry the fuck up with the methadone. Christ."

Maria dropped her sticks to help out. Theo stayed rooted in place.

"I was trying to learn more about magic, actually, so as to prevent said fuckups."

"Theo," Hanzo warned. "Leave it be."

"No, I'm not leaving it. Who put Blondie in charge anyway? Did I miss an election? If Sadhbh wants work from me, I want her respect. I'm not going to labour under these conditions. I'm not a dog."

"Fine. If you're not going to work, then go away. I'll be glad of the quiet."

"Well, what I mean is, I'm happy to help out. I'd like to help out, in fact. It's you that's getting in my way. Poor feedback leads to a loss of motivation, you know? It's bad management. Lack of incentives."

Sadhbh sucked in her cheeks, her eyes crystalline. "You want incentives for this?"

"Oh, don't pout at me," Theo retorted. "You know what I meant. Anyway, I'm a much better magician than I was a few weeks ago. The others can attest to that."

Hanzo hurried to unpack the methadone. Maria watched the argument unfold.

Sadhbh exhaled. "Listen, you gobshite. I didn't want you here in the first place, and you've been acting like a sullen child every time I give you a directive. We need an extra pair of hands, but we don't need a spoiled brat or a voluntourist. We're dealing with things much bigger than you. You need to act like it."

"I've been pulling my weight since Spain."

"Barely."

"Oh bloody hell, you think you're much better than me. So much higher and mightier. I won't be beholden to your superiority complex or whatever it is. I know your type. You pretend to be selfless, but you're only doing this for your ego. At least I'm honest."

Sadhbh snorted. "Believe whatever you want."

"In fact, logically, I must be a better magician than you because I'm less self-obsessed. If I walk away you won't know what you're missing. You're shooting yourself in the foot here."

Sadhbh ignored him. She just shook her head and resumed packing.

Theo's gut twisted. He was about to fly into a rage when Maria spoke up.

"Why don't the two of you have a race?"

"Very funny. Are you packed up?"

"I'm serious."

Sadhbh stopped and turned. Her eyes widened. "Oh god, you are."

Maria nodded. "Theo wants to prove himself, and you need to do something that isn't work. You can't always use other kinds of work to take a break from work, even if it's not so hard. You don't play many games these days. A race would be good for you."

"We need to sort out Brazil."

"We do, and we will. But this won't take forever. Give Theo, I don't know, a month to prepare, and we'll deal with this. Hanzo and I can organise the race in the meantime. Okay with you, Hanzo?"

Hanzo held up a hand. "Leave me out of this."

She shrugged, "Okay, I'll organise it then."

Sadhbh shook her head. "Forget it. Some other problems will appear. They always do."

"They do, but if I must listen to the two of you fighting any longer, the problem will be me."

"I really can't believe you're suggesting this."

"'You are not obligated to complete the work,'" Maria said, quoting something Theo didn't recognise, "'but neither are you free to desist from it.'"

"Exactly," Theo said, elated at the thought of challenging Sadhbh.

She laughed. "Alright. I'll agree to this farce. Theo?"

"Oh, I'm all in favour. But I want something if I win. I want to be the one giving the orders."

Sadhbh rolled her eyes. "I'm sure you do. If I win?"

"If you win, I'll do all supply runs myself."

"Hanzo already does most of them. I'd be more interested in you giving up drinking."

"Fine, no alcohol. I'll be a monk. It's not that big a sacrifice to me anyway you know."

"If there were any more of us..." Sadhbh folded her arms, her brows furrowed. "But there isn't. Fine. A race. You win, you can take charge. Give the orders. Route the supplies. Schedule the deliveries. See how long it lasts. If you lose, you know what you've promised. We're leaving you behind if you go back on any of this. You won't find us again. Got it?"

"Deal."

"One month. Until then, piss off and let us focus on the work."

Theo moved to leave. As he did so, Hanzo ran after him.

"Hey, wait, are you okay? Sadhbh said some pretty mean things there. I—"

"If you thought she was being cruel, then you should've corrected her."

"I... Yeah, I guess that's fair. My bad. I'm not good at those kinds of confrontations. Do you want help with your training or whatever, or—"

"No," said Theo. He seemed to look past Hanzo. "I already have some ideas of what to do. Right now, I feel like I should handle this on my own, and you should help in, where was it, Rio?"

"It's a lot to go train magic on your lonesome."

"I'm sure it is, but I'm one with the cosmos, remember?"

"Yeah," Hanzo said, studying him. "I remember."

"Good. Well then, if you'll excuse me, I have some reading to do."

Chapter Nine

*The abuse of symbolism is
like the abuse of food or
drink: it makes people ill,
and so their reactions become deranged.*

*——Alfred   Korzybski,
Science and Sanity*

To his credit, and to his debit, Theo trained hard. Following
Hanzo's original advice, he sought new knowledge to enhance
his magic. He knew he didn't understand music enough to support
the ritual foot-pounding he needed to perform. He decided he was
more of an instrumentalist than a stuffy theoretician.

Instead, he attempted to move through the world with politics,
figuring at first that there was a fundamental similarity between all
political struggles, which would expedite his Regardings. This proved
to be highly unreliable. The path from Berlin to Belfast was more
circuitous than he would have guessed, but the conceptual leap from

Belfast to Jerusalem was alarmingly short. Despite his confidence, he could not anticipate how different nations felt about their politics.

After ten days—over half lost in transit—and thirty espressos, he accepted this was a losing strategy.

Inspired by the bookshop in Maastricht, Theo next took to studying architecture. Addis Ababa might be deeply African, but it had skyscrapers the same as New York. Architecture would also let him leverage his faculty in working with toilets. Through nights and days spent secluded inside libraries, he picked up tools to cut through modest, bland buildings. Turns out the 'brut' in 'brutalism' refers to the French for 'raw,' as in raw concrete, rather than some form of violence inflicted upon the soul. The term 'brutalism' itself, however, originally came from Sweden, much like IKEA. Those concrete towers could guide Theo to modern interiors, like lines on a portolan chart.

Applying it to magic took a full week of study and nearly half a gram of speed.

His studies brought success. Now only a fifth of his time was lost, and new trails were revealed, ones laid down by the remarkable nobodies of the discipline. He would pick up and follow the recondite traces of one designer or another, walking through the failed cubicles of Robert Propst, the lacquered furnishings of Eileen Gray, or the fascist angles of Le Corbusier. He learned the Sears retail company used to mass produce houses in America and sell them in magazines. He could download the old catalogues onto his phone, cracking the country open like a ripe nut. Ditto worker monuments in the former USSR. Socialist realism had significant upsides vis-á-vis mass uniformity. By the end of the week, Theo could chew through raw concrete like fresh meat. Yet, he took no pleasure in his progress.

Maybe it was the drugs. Maybe it was because of them that he couldn't sleep. Maybe it was a deeper, more basic weakness that kept him awake. All his work—his study—demanded more of him than he had ever given to a task. He dug down deep into himself to find what reserves he had. A pit opened up within himself. There churned all the dark, oily, corrosive thoughts he never dared to dredge up. They began to leak into his waking mind.

He would lose. He wouldn't be fast enough. Sadhbh would destroy him, and when she destroyed him, Gabriel, Hanzo, and Maria would see him as the pathetic waste of skin he was. The bag of air puffed itself up so it could keep drifting along. The beggar. The failure. The leech.

If they saw him as that, then that's what he'd be. Things that are similar are the same.

The more he pressed himself, the more these thoughts seeped out, as if he were a sponge. They stained any joy he could find in his own progress. It didn't occur to him that, in another life, he would have made a good architect. It couldn't occur to him.

Instead, he took more drugs—to keep himself awake, to study harder, to fill the pit.

In the fourth and final week, he broke into the Home Office of the British government. A duplicated keycard brought him past their locks to the databases he needed. He found all of the personal and social information about himself he could. He found his national insurance number, tax history, medical records, and name and nationality. He looked, half in hope, for a missing person's report, but he didn't find one. He knew he wouldn't. He deleted every record he had access to, every trace of himself. It was a delirious, digital suicide. A form of occultation, of removing all the sympathetic ties that bound him. It was all dead semantic weight. It was all to be jettisoned.

When he left, he burned his passport upon a tyre fire in a scrap yard outside Bristol.

Theo didn't need these pitiable details. They were mere attachments. They could be deleted, expunged, reduced to ashes and fumes. He was bigger than them. He'd survive beyond them. Their destruction left him trembling with confidence.

As he stared into the heart of the fire, and watched his identity burn, he thought he saw a darkened shape. A sphere, a little bigger than his head, formed of impermeable blackness. The flames bent around it, as though heat or light could not apply to it. It hung there in the burning hearth, until the smoke stung Theo's eyes. When he blinked, it was no more, and he couldn't tell if it had ever been.

He was able to sleep afterwards. He rested a full night and a full day.

This was partially due to his confidence, but mostly due to downing benzos.

Rio de Janeiro was simple for Theo to reach. It was one of Le Corbusier's many failures. The urban planner had spent most of his life trying build his Radiant City: a rational, utopian dream where all citizens lived in grids of high-density housing, arranged in geometrical order, where transport to work was maximally efficient, and where said work was performed in massive high-rises. He had proposed razing the centre of Moscow to create it, and when he was rejected, proposed the same to Paris. He had tried and failed to create it in Barcelona, in Izmir, in Bogotá, and in many more besides, believing as he did that good city planning could only consist of strict regularity and standardisation. Many traces of him were left in the form of buildings, whether his own or those designed by students and colleagues.

Theo did not use them, however. He went through Algiers. Le Corbusier's failure there most closely resembled his failure in Rio, as both designs were meant to cope with sloping terrain along a waterfront.

Both even had viaducts.

They were to meet at the statue of *Cristo Redentor*, at the top of the city's hunchback mountain. Blue dawn cracked through the horizon, shimmering over sea mist and scattered islands, as Theo sauntered up the many steps. The soapstone lord was an Art Deco design, he observed. A convenient off-ramp for Paris, New York, or perhaps Vienna.

The sun stung his bloodshot eyes.

He took a slug from a bottle of water, where he had dissolved some MDMA, and placed a small tab of acid on his tongue. He relished the buzz at the back of his throat. The light, heady rush.

The others were already there, slouched against the parapet. Sadhbh unfurled her arms.

"You're late. Let's get this over with."

"Why rush?" Theo giggled. "Let's enjoy ourselves. Or are you afraid you'll lose?"

"Not a chance," she said. She squinted at him. "Are you alright?"

"Never better, mon capitaine."

"Okay. Well. Maria, if you would."

Maria stepped forward. "The format is as follows. We will draw lots from a set of destinations to decide the route. We will give each person a piece of chalk, which they will use to show they have been there. You will mark a given public building at your destination, but each of you will have different buildings. You will then text us an image of your mark. You will be told if you arrived first or second."

Sadhbh looked sidelong at him, "Good with you?"

"Hold your horses, oh Catherine the Great. Will someone verify the marks?"

"You think I'd cheat?"

"No, but I think you'll accuse me of cheating when you lose."

Hanzo sighed, "Yeah, sure. One of us will go check after the text."

"Good with me." Theo began jumping up and down and boxed the air.

Sadhbh chewed her lips. "This is silly."

"That's the point," Maria said. "Do you want to forfeit?"

"No," she growled.

Once the route was drawn, the runners were given fifteen minutes to consider their paths. Their destinations were a mix of remote tourist locales, which demanded broad geographic awareness. Theo pulled out a sheaf of notes he had scrawled over the last month, but he was unable to read them. He had to stop himself from telling everyone he was going to win. The joy in his veins told him he should. He was Gabriel's gift to them. The musician in him said he should give them a show.

When the time elapsed, the runners went down to the restaurant at the foot of the statue. They were handed their chalk, and Maria texted the first set of buildings. The race began.

The runners faced three key problems. First: knowledge of the places to move towards. For all Theo's abuse of intoxicants, he did at least retain a memory for places, scaffolded further by videos and panoramas available online. Second: connecting the place they were in to where they were going. This was where his architectural learnings, aided by the high he was riding, came into play. Third: the time lag which occurred as they hopped hither and thither, and about which he could do bupkis.

When the race started, Theo ran to the nearest public restroom as fast as he could. He found and dragged a metal rubbish bin inside, placing it under the handle to deny it to Sadhbh. She, for her part, sat back on a bench and watched him run.

Theo slammed into a toilet stall, screwed his eyes shut, and Regarded the design of sanitation systems of coastal urban centres in South America. Soon, he shot out of another toilet at Punta del Este, Uruguay. He sprinted through the sunny resort town, taking multiple wrong turns until he placed his signature on a secluded spot on the town hall, where he was sure it wouldn't be washed away. He sent his snapshot.

First, the reply read. He pumped his fist in the air.

Through further gleanings of coastal architecture, he reached Vernazza, Italy, where he maintained his lead. Here, his strategy backfired. His next hop brought him to Monterosso, a similar town within the Cinque Terre region. Though it felt like five minutes, he had spent hours of real-time going in the wrong direction. His path was saved by the mountainous landscape, which helped him in his route to the alpine city of Ifrane, Morocco.

It was in Zermatt, Switzerland, that he started to lag.

Second, the text read, after he marked a pillar outside the Matterhorn Museum.

Second, the text read, when he was leaving Lofoten, Norway.

Second, it said again, in Chott el Djerid, Tunisia.

Second, second, second.

There was more than half the race left to run. Sweat streamed down him as he ran from waypoint to waypoint. He didn't know by how much he was losing. He didn't know how to regain his position. He didn't know how he would look Sadhbh in the eyes when he lost.

He did not know how he could justify the time he spent if it all ended in failure.

His chemical confidence evaporated. Dark, lurid waves swelled within him. They lapped at his awareness. They made the world swim, bringing him from vertiginous crests to deep troughs.

Panic was a black flower blooming, watered by lysergic acid.

A vine, cracking through walls of concrete.

Life, which refuses to be denied.

Theo did all he could not to think about failure, and yet thoughts of failing, of being kicked aside, of being judged and abandoned, broke through the surge barrier of his mind. Theo ran on and these thoughts, in their great charcoal forms, followed him. They overtook him, they curled around him, and, finally, they swallowed him up.

Chapter Ten

> But there is more, and
> worse, to come: this life must
> be 'made nothingness' so
> that the secret of existence
> may be revealed, name-
> ly nothingness, the noth-
> ingness within every man,
> his 'infinite' ability to free
> himself from any instant,
> any moment, any state,
> any determined situation,
> in and through nothing-
> ness.
>
> —Henri Lefebvre, Critique
> of Everyday Life

The Fushimi Inari shrine, Japan. The sky is pink. Great red
wooden arches stretch out before him. They are an infinity

mirror cutting up the base of a mountain whose name he does not know.

The air is cold. He knows he is going to lose this race.

From this knowledge more knowledge springs.

He knows what people say about him. He can't push it aside any longer. He knows he'll be no great philosopher. He knows he'll never be an artist of any renown. He knows he won't make a difference. He knows nobody will care about him. He knows nobody likes him. He can't even manage to be a good friend or a good student. He knows he does not and will not matter, and that all the times he indulged in fantasy were an attempt to hold this fact at bay.

He's a person of almosts. Almost a musician. Almost a magician. Almost a person.

Every person has their place, he tells himself, and you've always abandoned yours. The bridges are burned, and there's nowhere to go. Your parents don't want you and your country doesn't know you. Gabriel said you impressed him, but be honest with yourself. He was lying. You have no talent. You can achieve nothing. You were just some annoying guy he was obligated to care for because you smashed your own face into concrete because you're an idiot. He pawned you off onto the others as yet another charity case, and fuck, if you haven't spent months hanging around, unable to be anything less than useless.

Scrounger. Obligate parasite.

Let's face it: the folks in Berlin had the right idea, shutting you out. Larissa was a saint.

At least you didn't challenge her to a race. What are you, twelve? Why are you doing this? Do you have any clue how many people could use that minute speck of magical ability you have? Do you have even the faintest notion how many people have it worse than you? Somehow, despite your tours, you don't.

Ungrateful little scrote.

But it's not like a weak, useless idiot like you could do anything about their lives.

As if you could solve any of the problems out there. Give over.

You deserve to be on your own. Why did Gabriel spend any time with you?

By rights, you should piss off and die. Sadhbh was polite to you.

Just finish this race so the others don't think you've fucked off out of laziness again.

Show up and let them rip you apart like you deserve.

A seething hot anger arises within him. It starts to strip away all his acid-burnt thoughts. All his excuses, all his denials, all that was secondary or ancillary peeled away under the glare of righteous self-hatred. His ego burned in the furnace of his chest. His blood fumed. His fingernails raked across the flesh of his palms, and the pressure within him searched for a release.

As Theo burned, he viewed himself anew. He saw himself as another interchangeable body.

He saw himself as nothing. He Regarded himself as nothing.

He scoured himself of sympathy.

Then, he accelerated to the next destination, to finish the race.

All things are bound by sympathy.

Therefore, nothing cannot be bound by sympathy.

When Theo returned to Rio, he was greeted by Maria and Hanzo.

The shock in their eyes told him all he needed to know.

"Sadhbh isn't here," he said.

Maria shook her head. "You arrived at Gaborone just before her."

Theo stared up into the shadowy figure of *Cristo Redentor*. "I did it then."

"I guess you did." Hanzo reached out to shake his hand. "Congrats, man."

Theo didn't take it. He seemed unaware of it.

Hanzo scratched his cheek and gave a quick laugh. "Y'know, Sadhbh could be another couple hours, maybe more. We could get something to eat. They got some pretty good hamburgers here—"

Hanzo stopped talking as Sadhbh crested the steps to the statue. She halted upon seeing Theo. She took a moment to collect herself, and then walked up to him.

He bristled, waiting for a vicious remark or worse, but she struck out her hand.

"You win. Congratulations. It was a good race."

"Was it, now?"

She nodded. "We should do more of them. They'd be good training."

"They would."

She retracted her hand. "Well, I'll uphold the bet. You're in charge now. What are your instructions?"

Theo glared at her. She was taking this far too well. He had imagined his moment of triumph to be something rendered dramatically, with epic orations extolling his brilliance. He had imagined it changing something in his heart, but this wasn't it. It wasn't changing it. It wasn't changing anything.

"Oh, don't pretend you aren't annoyed. I beat you fair and square."

"I know you did. What more do you want? You're faster than me. Okay."

"No, you're annoyed I beat you, and you can't accept it."

"What are you talking about?" she asked. "Look, one of us is going to be faster than the other. Could have been you, could have—"

"It is me."

"I know, for fuck's sake. Can you get over yourself for one second?"

"Yeah, you hate that someone so sad and pathetic as me beat you."

"Jesus, Theo. You're faster than me, fine, I accept it. I'm annoyed I didn't win, but if you're better than me, fine. You can help more people than I can. I raced so you'd focus on the work afterwards and—"

"Why? You want to shout at me more and tell me how shit a leader I am too?"

Sadhbh bit her lip and nodded. "Okay, that's fair. I'm sorry I—"

"Sorry? God, you're so full of shit. I know you're not sorry. Folks like you are never sorry."

"Theo," Maria whispered. "Calm down. You're acting very stra—"

"Oh enough," Theo snapped. "All this charity work is bullshit. It's pointless, and it doesn't matter, and it doesn't count for anything. No matter what we do, it's all the fucking same. It never fucking changes. The only reason to do it is so you can feel good about yourselves, so you can look down on all the people who didn't get magic. That's why you all do it. It's pure condescension, a—a pretend altruism. That's why we're here, skiving off and calling it rest or training or whatever lies we're telling ourselves, instead of dealing with what's really going on in this world, because we know we can't do anything meaningful about it. And I've—I've needed people like you before, but you were never there, because I'm not interesting enough. I know I'm not. Certainly not next to the ability to mumble at USB sticks all day, or do fun little break-ins, or read neuroscience textbooks, or bang on fucking tree stumps. I survived, though, without people like you. And this is the result. I'm a better magician because I'm honest about how useless this all is and because I don't go off on an ego trip, dropping yoghurts off on street corners and calling it self-sacrifice. I'm the only one here who isn't deluding themselves. I am not going back to making silly little inventories so I can traipse off into crisis zones and tell myself I'm helping and doing some noble duty. I'm not. You can, but I'm out."

Theo's rant was met with silence, and the other three magicians watched him with the same demeaning eyes so many others had in his life, so many others who just wanted him to shut up. Theo decided he had spoken truth to power. He went to leave.

"Wait. Please stay. I would like you to stay," Maria said.

Theo turned on her, full of unspecified rage. "Oh, and why is that?"

"Because I think if you leave now, you'll hurt yourself."

"Maria put it blunter than I could," Hanzo said. "I want you to stay too pal. Hey Sadhbh? Say something. C'mon."

Sadhbh's stony expression gave way to a deep, worn tiredness. "I'll finish saying what I wanted to say earlier. Theo, I *am* sorry I was harsh to you before. I was too hard on you."

This remark was the final straw.

"I don't need your fucking pity," he snarled.

He turned and walked away, out of the lives of the enclave. They called after him, but he ignored them. His eyes glinted white with nihilistic, misanthropic pride. He had the taste of a saccharine victory on his lips. He wouldn't tell Gabriel about this. The man had abandoned him, so what right had he to hear of Theo's successes? Nah, the new mage had learned to break the rules, which made him the master of them.

He knew he was nothing. He knew he could do anything.

Chapter Eleven

Our world, like a char-
nel-house, is strewn with the
detritus of dead epochs.

—Le Corbusier, Towards a
New Architecture

In his invulnerable enlightenment, Theo decided to push his magic
as far as it would go. He wanted to be everywhere, all at once, in
an apotheosis of apathy. He wanted to whet his knowledge to a bloody
edge. He wanted to smear himself across the landscape like a car crash
victim.

He went back to architecture, starting with monuments. You could
get to the Arc de Triomphe through Brandenburger Tor, and the
Reichstag was a neoclassical stone's throw from the White House.
From monuments, he went through to history. Jerusalem taught him
antiquity's steps. Following them, he came to Cairo, to Istanbul and
Rome, cities which inhabited their own ruins. Their doors opened to
Timbuktu, Kaifeng and Cusco. All the world's centuries were com-
pressed into days.

He never stood still. He moved everywhere and stayed nowhere. He fled the sun and lived in eternal night. He spoke to no one. He stole whatever he needed. He barely rested, barely comprehended the places he travelled to beyond their role as nodes in his network. In the span of weeks, he acquired skills which took most magicians years. He could shout from the Matterhorn and hear his echo at K2. He infiltrated the homes of billionaires and government offices, simply to prove he could. Simply to be everywhere.

Guadalajara, Dalian, Khartoum, Belo Horizonte. Names, words, syllables. Smelt them down through semantic satiation; they don't matter. Nowhere matters. Everywhere is all alike. Things which are similar are the same. Everywhere is the same. Details only serve to anchor you. Don't let the sensual get its hooks into you. Let everywhere blur together. Move as a blur through everywhere.

He was nothing.

He was indistinguishable from the universe.

He was the universe.

He was a spectre, haunting the ends of the earth for his own ends.

If, in all his frantic flitting, there was ever a risk of encountering the enclave again, he would leave. He couldn't stomach greeting them. He couldn't even stand to observe them from afar. The enclave pretended their sacrifices were for some holy cause, that lowly punks and runaways could somehow push back the dial on the doomsday clock, but Theo knew all their names would be consigned to dust, and all their works would amount to a Mecca *de nada*.

The fire in his chest never died down, no matter how hotly he burned. He couldn't escape the searing pain of it, as he strove to make himself ever more efficient. He viewed himself with the coldest, steeliest gaze he could muster, harder and crueller than anything Sadhbh had ever said and yet there was always more sympathy to remove, more ties to cut. Still, he took some comfort in knowing that his name would be lost to time too. That certainty gave him solace, even as his mania began to rip him apart.

He was in Auckland when he started unmooring.

At first, it wasn't entirely obvious. It came upon him as whispers, the kind that come with lack of sleep. The kind heard when one thinks a friend has said something they haven't. The little twists and curlicues of thought inside the brain, just past the ear. He thought he heard a pigeon caw like a crow. Then the engines of cars sounded like the strumming of a guitar. And sometimes, when people spoke, they shifted into accents that weren't their own.

He wrote it off as an effect of the drugs he was taking. Amphetamines and psychedelics aren't an anxiolytic blend, so red-eyed Theo decided to go cold turkey. It didn't help. There'd been too hard a push, too fast, with too many chemical aids. The aftermath of the amphetamines left him a zombie, exhausted yet unable to sleep, and though he persevered, the whispers didn't quieten down. Soon, he could hear the conversations of pedestrians from across the road, as though they spoke directly to him. He tried listening to music to block them out, but one track would morph into another track or another genre entirely. The whispers stretched out into his peripheral vision. Lights shimmered with iridescent auras, and patterned surfaces swam. When he looked at the corners of buildings, he could see around them.

The little whispers told him what was happening. His mind was warping like melted plastic. In trying to fold the world's atlas into a postage stamp, in trying to connect every point to every other point, everything was becoming an analogy for everything else. There would be no things distinct in themselves. There would be no discrete objects, only sets of unstable metaphors, fluid, streaming, dissipating.

The little whispers told him all this. He tried to push through them. It didn't help.

He sensed strange, phantom fingers picking at his skin, plucking at his muscles. Their touches felt like the twitches of an epileptic, or an alcoholic suffering withdrawal. He drank harder to make sure it wasn't that, to keep the fear down. But the phantom impulses spread and grew in intensity.

In Saint Petersburg, his hands turned into alien, wandering creatures running their fingers through his hair and into his mouth. In Busan, he was walking across a railway bridge when his feet jerked and almost threw him down onto the line beneath. In Johannesburg, his neck twisted as he crossed a busy street. He collapsed onto the road. He tried to pick himself up, but he started walking in the opposite direction to where he intended. Motor signals cross-fired in his brain, and nausea overcame him. He vomited onto the footpath. In the mire of egested acid, he saw a splatter of green ribbon noodles. He couldn't remember ever eating any.

He took refuge under a bridge along the Juksei River, unable to move, shivering and dry-heaving.

When the whispers addressed him, he would reply aloud without restraint or even an understanding of what he was saying. There were times he'd black out and come to, meters away from where he'd been. He would see half-images of people he recognised in others on the street, in the walls, in the water. He'd recognise people he had never met before. His mood, too, shifted wildly, going from elation to despair to rage. His inner monologue stopped being his own, splintering into duologues and tetralogues. There were times he convinced himself these other voices were his own, but he'd lose his convictions within the hour.

There was one situation in which he regained control of himself. When dozens of concerned eyes were on him, his body and mind solidified, and he could move them as he wished. When he lashed out in furious panics, he attracted attention, and the attention calmed him down. To stay sane, he had to be seen. He had to be localised, whether in Johannesburg, or Jakarta, or Juneau, or wherever the hell.

After three nights underneath the Joburg bridge, he huddled his knees up to his chest and prayed. He brought to mind all the warnings which had ever been levied against him, by Sadhbh, by Gabriel, and by those from his life before, and he asked for forgiveness.

"I'm sorry," his voice cracked. "I'm so sorry. I don't know what's wrong with me. I don't know how to fix myself. I keep fucking up, but I don't know what to do. I need an out. Please. I don't deserve it, but please. Give me an out."

With that prayer he disappeared.

Chapter Twelve

*How is it that we never
reach the ideal? It's because
it would annihilate itself.*

——*Novalis, Fragments*

Theo appeared just outside a small fishing village in Cambodia, under the shadow of tall tropical trees. Their leaves split the sunlight, dappling the brown sands before him. The humidity bore down, heavy and sticky as fear. The sound of birdsong pressed in from all angles. The whispers gave them a bizarre reverb.

He started, and instinctively checked his phone before studying his surroundings.

The village nearby was full of colourful wooden buildings painted bright blue or turquoise. Long jetties stretched out into the sea, providing anchorage for humble crafts given the same bright paint. He could make out a newly built monastery in the distance, with an entrance marked by colonnettes and a wide-painted lintel. It was a quiet place.

He knew why he was here. This was enclave territory. The shame of how he had acted towards them overwhelmed him, and he slammed his eyes shut, reactively trying to muster another way out. Only, the black panic came back.

The whispers rose. The twitches stirred his muscles. Theo lost what little control he had left.

His consciousness split apart, several times over, like worn fabric finally tearing apart.

His awareness was distributed throughout the village. Several images appeared to him in an anaglyphic storm. All at once, he saw people haggling in the village market, bright parrots in the trees, fish swimming in the blue beyond, and every time he tried to move his eyes new images would appear. He was an insect, with compound eyes and compound ears, crushed by sensations pressing in at all sides. He tried to cry out with a mouth he could no longer locate, and when he searched for it, he received visions of Laos, Vietnam, and Thailand.

A voice cut through the rush, "Theo?"

The voice brought him back towards himself, but not completely. The scene remained fractured, stitched from multiple perspectives. He saw his body on the sand, lying foetal, eyes wide and blank, lips gibbering silent protests. He recognised the woman standing over him. The heavy dreadlocks frizzed with humidity. It was Maria.

"You've lost your mind." Her voice echoed throughout him. "Poor boy."

She crouched down and placed her hands on his shoulders. She gazed at him as though he were the vessel for a spirit.

"Theo, you are a good person. You have a funny sense of humour when you aren't so insecure and trying so hard to be funny. You are not a great guitar player, but you practise very rarely, so this is not a surprise. You only play guitar because you think it is the coolest instrument. You are a hard worker when you care and when you think nobody is looking. You are selfish and you sometimes say such bitter things, but I think it's because you're afraid. You want to be special, and you are afraid that if you are not then people won't care about you. You don't need to be afraid."

Her eyebrows wrinkled, trying to fish for words. "Also, your hair is very badly maintained. You think it is cool, but it isn't. You are going bald. You look like someone cut off the end of a mop and put it on your head. Your beard is patchy too. You'd look better with it shaven. Also, you need to wash more. You smell like tomato soup most days. Your breath smells of it all the time. I don't know if you actually eat so much tomato soup, but this is the smell."

As she described Theo, he drew back into himself. Her attention solidified him. His eyes fluttered, and now his vision came through them. His mouth clacked open and closed. Every muscle in his body felt exhausted, as after weightlifting or a seizure. They had been ripping themselves apart, he realised.

"Maria?" he said to the face above.

"Yes, it's me. Is your mind back where it belongs? Are you seeing me with your eyes?"

Theo flushed. He didn't know what to say.

She ran her hands over him like a doctor, checking his pulse, his breathing. "Has this happened to you before?"

He laughed. His voice was faint, his throat hoarse.

"Oh, you know, off and on. It's a way to spend the evenings."

"Yes, if this was the second or third time, you probably would be dead." She wrinkled her nose. "You've pissed yourself. And maybe something worse. You'll need to be cleaned up, and then you'll need rest."

Theo held back a quip. Instead, he propped himself upright as if to prove to Maria that he wasn't seriously sick or injured. His arm trembled under his weight.

"Tell me something," he asked. "Did you know the woman who went to the moon?"

"This isn't the time for stories."

"I want to know—was she real? Could we really leave Earth if we tried?"

Maria pressed her mouth into a thin frown. "Yes. I knew her."

"Did she make it back?"

Her expression shifted into a strange mixture of sadness and pride. "She did."

"Can I meet her?"

"No. You will never meet that person. Once she came back, she said she would never touch the world of illusion again. When she went to the moon, she expected to find something there, but there was nothing. She saw rocks and grey dust and cold, empty darkness. She saw the moon, and it was simply the moon. She lost years of life learning this fact. In a sense, magic had killed her moon, and left her with only the Earth. So, she wants to live there now, instead. She says the view of it is beautiful."

"The others are nearby," she said, after a long pause. "We have spare trousers. You'll come say hello and get changed. You can apologise when you're there."

"Thanks, but I—"Maria grabbed hold of his shirt and shoved him back down to the ground.

"This is not a discussion."

Theo and Maria went deep inside the sweltering forest, where the thrum of insects swelled and their clothes stuck to their skin. Theo dragged his feet the whole way along. Every step of his seemed to find a new branch to crack, though the sounds were at least undistorted.

"Don't make me do this," he said. "They won't want to see me."

"What did I say before?"

"Yes, but I'll only be a nuisance."

The trees thinned out into a small clearing. There was little more than a couple of stray hammocks strung up with netting and sprayed down with repellent, but the enclave was there. He saw the glint of a smoky flame. Sat upon some stones beside it were Sadhbh and Hanzo, reading.

"Everyone," said Maria. "Theo is back."

Sadhbh put her book down. Her white hair hung down over her eyes.

Maria pulled him out of the undergrowth. He stood before them, shamefaced. A guy at a party who's drank too much. His guts coiled within him, and he couldn't stammer out a single word.

Hanzo sniffed. "Pull up a chair, dipshit. Do you want food? We got rice."

He hadn't eaten in days. He wasn't sure if he was hungry.

"Wait," said Maria. She went to a hammock and retrieved a pair of sweatpants, a five-litre jug of water, and a packet of tissues. She thrust these into Theo's arms. Then she pointed. "You can clean up over there."

"Whose trousers are these? If they're for delivery, I won't take—"

"They're for someone in need."

Once out of sight, Theo stripped, washed himself down, and covered his soiled clothes with dirt. They were close to rags regardless. He patted himself dry with tissue paper and put on the sweatpants. They were a few inches too short.

What were the odds he could escape from them on foot if he bolted into the treeline? How far would he get? If he returned to the village, then the other people there could block their magic. He could teleport again. Go to the Amazon maybe. It felt similar to here.

All delusions. Fantasies. His magic would rip him apart again if he teleported. His prayers had been answered, and now he had to face providence.

The insects and the birds were loud enough to conceal the sob which escaped from him.

He returned to the camp once he had time to wipe away his tears. His footsteps cut off their whispered conversation, and he slumped down onto the ground by the fire. He risked only sparing glances at Hanzo and Sadhbh. He felt as loud as an exploding amp.

"You want that food or nah?" Hanzo asked him.

"No, thank you. Don't cook on my account."

Sadhbh got up. She fetched a bowl and scraped some rice and beans into it from a large cooking pot off to the side. She passed it to him.

"Eat it before it gets cold," she said. Her face was calm, and her voice even.

Theo nodded and ate. Nobody spoke as he did so. Hanzo and Sadhbh returned to their reading, while Maria began boiling water for tea on a small gas stove. The food was both bland and salty.

The whispers called out to him as he ate. They washed out any other sounds he could hear. He tried not to draw attention to himself, waiting for the phantom force to fade. Then, the foreign impulses seized his muscles and his arm twitched, flicking a spoonful of oily rice onto Sadhbh's cheek.

Everyone looked at Theo. Theo looked at his spoon.

"You guys aren't in the mood for a food fight then," he said.

Sadhbh wiped her cheek clean. "How do you feel?" she asked.

"No worse than usual."

"And how long have you been feeling that way?"

"Okay. Maybe I have been feeling a little worse recently. Maybe I'm coming down with something. Don't think it's contagious, though. Some metaphysical aches and pains. A little ontological ague. All I need is a hot toddy."

He expected Sadhbh to roll her eyes, or huff and turn back to reading, or some other indication of her lack of patience with him and his bad jokes. She didn't. She pursed her lips, and her eyes creased.

"No, you won't be alright. You're losing yourself."

The air weighed Theo down. He drew tighter into himself.

"Fine. Fine. What does that mean, then?"

Maria answered. "The sympathies of others are controlling you. You are feeling their emotions, sensing what they sense. Their experiences are overwriting yours. This is what happens when you're too sympathetically removed." She shook her head. "We should have stopped you."

"It's self-abasement," Hanzo added. "Older magicians, way back, thought it meant they were getting closer to God or whatever. It was a religious experience. They were getting themselves out of the way so they could receive enlightenment."

"Well, I don't want anything to do with any god," Theo snapped. "I don't want this at all. I want to be left alone. How can I cure it?"

"There are no quick solutions at all, at least none that I know of. No pill to swallow. It's only ever happened to a few folks that I've heard of."

There was a lull in the conversation, and Hanzo prodded Sadhbh with his foot.

"Come on. Tell him about it."

Sadhbh sighed. "Thanks for that."

"It happened to you?"

She brushed her hair back from her forehead. "Yeah. It was early after I found magic. In Ireland, I lived in what you'd call a Magdalene Laundry. These were workhouses run by nuns. They sent you there if you were a 'problem girl.' Originally that meant prostitutes, but then it meant unmarried mothers, victims of abuse, those with a disability or a mental illness. On and on. There didn't have to be much of a reason to be sent. You'd leave one abusive household, then you'd go to another kind in the Laundries. They'd make sure you knew why you were there. They'd work you to the bone, humiliate you. Try to make you feel grateful that you had a bed at all. They didn't care a whit for you though. They've been finding mass graves belonging to women and children who went to these places. On and off for the last thirty years."

Her expression grew distant for a moment, and then she returned. "Anyway. Long time ago now. I don't know how old I am in personal-time, but in real years, I'm going on sixty-five. I was after running away from one when I tapped into magic. Smashed a window and ran, thinking I wanted to be anywhere but there. There's probably still a nun out there who thinks I died in the cold. Met Gabriel after that, in Canada, near one of their schools for First Nations people. He was already doing some enclave work there, so I joined him. I didn't really know how to be a person when I started. I still don't, in fairness. A lot of the guilt drilled into me... it stuck. I have a hard time thinking about all the people in need of help. I worked myself too hard at the start, and sure enough, a couple of years into it, I went your way. I started disintegrating. I've gotten better at cutting myself some slack, but it took effort, and I'm not always the best at it."

"How bad did it get?"

She smacked her tongue against her palate. "I was bedridden at the worst of it. Couldn't walk in a straight line. Heard voices from all over. Skin started splitting, blistering. Literally coming apart at the seams. I think was able to walk after a month or so, but I didn't shake it for two years. Maybe longer."

"Two years."

"Yeah. Two years of not being able to do anything, or very little. Gabriel regretted allowing me to push myself so hard. Said he was sorry. His advice was that I shouldn't do any magic until I'd gone three months without voices. He knew someone who died from them. Fell down in traffic. Though, three months wasn't enough time for me. Brought everything right back. I think it's the sort of thing where, when you get it, it stays with you, and you have to manage it for the rest of your life. It's why I prefer to do the scheduling these days."

Theo's neck twitched, bringing his face up into a painful rictus. He forced his head down in a strained gyrating motion.

"Hey," Sadhbh said. Theo's gaze snapped to her.

"We'll help you out until you get better."

"It's two years. I can't stay with you for two years."

"You need the help."

"After all the shit I said? You want me clinging to you like, I don't know, like some tumour?"

"Yes. I was trying so hard to see everything that I lost sight of you, and I hurt you. If I can't treat the people around me decently, then how can I hope to help strangers? I owe you, and I think the others agree."

Maria and Hanzo both nodded.

"Read the room Theo," Sadhbh said. "I know you're bad at it but do it this time."

"I'll only get in your way. You'll be teleporting all over for deliveries."

"You're not planning on staying here, are you? You can move and we can move."

Theo didn't answer. He realised the matter had been decided while he was changing his clothes.

Sadhbh gave a tired chuckle. "You're a real gobshite sometimes, you know that?"

"Yeah. I know. I'm sorry about that, for what it's worth."

Chapter
Thirteen

We cannot step beyond the
everyday. The marvellous
can only continue to exist
in fiction and the illusions
that people share. There is
no escape. And yet we wish
to have the illusion of escape
as near to hand as possible.

—Henri Lefebvre, Critique
of Everyday Life

Without a passport, leaving Cambodia took him a week. The enclave had visited the country to drill holes into the boats of traffickers heading to nearby Thailand, and after negotiating with a fisherman, they arranged for him to leave by a similar route. They decided the best course would be for him to return to Berlin. It was where he knew the most people and where he might have a better chance of finding housing. This plan would require him to travel over 11,000 kilometres through multiple national borders.

The enclave didn't bother admonishing him about his passport. They gave him travel supplies. A rucksack filled with food and water. A tarp for the rain. Sunscreen, map, and compass. A GPS tracker. A sleeping bag. Spare shoes, spare clothes.

The kinds of things they would provide for others in need. Things he had once helped to source.

It was a kindness repaid.

They checked in on him periodically. Often this was a simple exchange of texts. They avoided discussing magic with him, preferring to talk about books and films or play a game together. Sadhbh taught Theo a few card games, and they played chess asynchronously over their phones. She was pretty good at it. More competitive than Theo would have guessed. Or perhaps he was surprised she played with him at all.

Sometimes, when they visited, they'd teleport to somewhere a few dozen miles off his course, and he'd have to adjust. His detours could be long and arduous, but they were necessary to obtain more food, extra clothing, or whatever else he needed. He depended wholly on the enclave for his survival. Maria was the one who usually visited. She took the lead in researching holes in border security and shepherding him through. The enclave even made sure he could rest in a few scattered hostels along the way, paying for proper beds without thought. It was a small, minor thing. Of no consequence. *De nada*.

With every kindness given to him, Theo felt worse.

It ate away at him as he hiked and hitchhiked the long miles, telling drivers he was just another random Westerner on a gap year. Though the whispers quieted, they weren't silent. They stayed with him, and in a strange sense, he relished them. They, and the distortions they brought, heightened reality. They were of an emotional intensity that, however painful, was more dramatic than the life which lay before him.

He knew this was a terrible belief. He knew his years must be left fallow. He felt ashamed of the feeling, just as he felt ashamed of his dependence, but he couldn't let go of it. The mortification pulled on him harder than any pack as he travelled through Bangladesh, into India, into Pakistan and beyond.

"Hey Maria. Can you tell me more about those spirits?"

The four of them sat in a café in Diyarbakır, Turkey. It was a charming building, finished in colourful ashlars with an old wagon wheel propped up against the front wall, tucked in amongst the generic high-rises Theo knew so intimately. It had been three months since he started walking. They were marking the occasion.

"I remember you telling me about them. Hopefully, it doesn't feel so long for you." Theo jabbed a fork into his *künefe*, breaking through the syrup-soaked pastry into soft cheese. Whatever else might be said about his condition, he was glad to be able to eat local food again.

Maria lit up, but Hanzo cut her off.

"Not sure you sure you wanna hear about these things," he said.

"No, I do. I never learned about spirits, and they seemed rather fun. No doubt Maria had a whole spiel lined up. Sadhbh and I had our argument just as it got going, and then it was off to the races, so to speak."

"It still doesn't feel like the right conversation for the day."

"Well, I'll defer to Sadhbh then. What do you think?"

Sadhbh smiled and poured milk into her tea. "Go ahead, Maria."

"With pleasure. Which ones should I speak about?"

"Tell me about the dangerous ones," Theo said. "That's where we left off."

Maria placed her cup back on her saucer. Her voice went low and conspiratorial. She enjoyed the theatrics. "Okay. I'll tell you about the most dangerous spirit, which is also the oldest kind I know. This is a beast that kills any magicians it encounters. It can be sensed before it is met, which gives you time to run away, but you do not hide from the beast. It can always find a magician lost in its habitat, and hunts them down. This beast goes by many names. It's called the Place-Eater, the Ortgeist, or Guth an Bothán."

"Ah, this one," Sadhbh said. "Got joke names too. Gabriel called it the Hotelnivore."

"Just so," Maria continued. "The Place-Eater is found in abandoned places, or places where there are many similar buildings, but almost no people. Ghost towns. Run-down motels. Derelicts. Derelict is the perfect word for the places they haunt. The larger, the more dangerous. Detroit has some, but they say the worst of them resides in Pripyat."

Hanzo smirked. "I've never heard of this. Sounds like radiation poison or something."

"Who's to say? Have you heard of the Glasgow effect?"

He scratched his jaw. "Can't say I have."

"It's a statistical fact. There is a tendency for people to die younger in Glasgow than anywhere else in Europe. You can include poverty and health and so on in your analysis, but there will still be this higher mortality. Experts, who know nothing about magic, have a theory. They say it's caused by living near derelict land. You see, some architects said Glasgow shouldn't have tenements. They were overcrowded, and unhealthy to live in, and so they should be replaced with tower apartments. So, the city tore down its tenements. This destroyed the communities in the city, which made everyone living in them more vulnerable to all kinds of stresses. Derelict land indicates a site where this destruction occurred, and I think you will find Place-Eaters there, chewing on people."

To his surprise, Theo knew about this. Le Corbusier was the main inspiration for the plan. Similarly, residents of Brasília, which had mostly been built on his principles, had a term for the psychological effect of living there without the sense of community found in other cities. He wondered if Chandigarh also had a term, as that was the one city he actually built.

He kept quiet, however. Maria knew more than he did about what mattered.

"How does the beast form?" he asked.

"Scraps of sympathy," Maria said. "Everything has sympathetic connections to everything else, no? They can be weak, but they are always there. Imagine a family staying in a room in a bad motel. Room 101 or so, no matter. Let's say these are the first visitors in a long time. Naturally, each room in the motel is made to be identical. By the law of sympathy, this means the family is in all of the other rooms too, because they are so similar. They are in 102 and 103 and so on. By being in each of these rooms, they leave echoes of themselves behind. Traces of a trace of themselves. These are the scraps of sympathy."

"You can think of them like dust," Sadhbh said. "Motes of person-ality. Emotional dandruff. As Gabe put it to me, it's not unlike how magicians will mark a place to connect themselves to it."

Hanzo frowned. "Didn't know you were into spirits too."

She sipped on her tea. "I have some respect for this one."

"Well, even so, these scraps gotta be real weak. Much weaker than any kind of sigil."

"Yep. In the real world, you have people to-ing and fro-ing all over the shop. There's no time for them to settle anywhere. They don't do anything. Just sediments of soul."

"But in abandoned places," Theo said, deep in thought. "They can collect."

Maria nodded. "Imagine next that a couple is going to the motel. Maybe they're running away together; maybe it is a romantic road trip. They arrive after the family has left. Room 101 has been cleaned, so they'll take that one. Now, the scraps in Room 101 have been moved by the house master's presence, by their thoughts, feelings, and actions. But their presence is not so strong in the other rooms, so the scraps there will stay, and new scraps will join them. There aren't enough people at this motel to fill the other rooms, so they receive more scraps, more, and more, and so on. Dust is a good comparison because, like dust, these scraps will come together. We don't know why. Maybe it's like the electric field, like magnetism. Maybe it's an instinct that sympathetic connections have to reach out to each other. But they will make something with a shape and a kind of consciousness. Not a real consciousness, but something with a hunger. A beast made of abandonment. This is the Place-Eater. To grow, it feeds on other scraps, on the parts of people they leave behind. It tries to keep its habitat homogenous, to make more scraps to feed on."

"How does it kill? Does it literally eat magicians?"

"It rips you apart," Sadhbh said. "Eats you. Digests you. Magic relies on you being sympathetically removed. That leaves you vulnerable to it."

"They really devour you? Just like that?"

"Yes," Maria said. "You should talk to—"

"Maria." Sadhbh shot across her.

"Oh. Sorry. Never mind."

"I shouldn't talk to whom?" Theo asked.

"Never you mind." Sadhbh reached over and patted his hand. "Do you want another *künefe*? Another coffee? We don't have to rush off anywhere. I made sure."

"No, hang on. Is it Gabriel? You've mentioned him a few times. Is he an expert on these things?"

Sadhbh blushed, her neck reddening in blotches. "Yes. To the extent any magician can be."

"To what extent, then?"

"Well... He's the only one of us known to have beaten a Place-Eater."

Theo sat back in his chair and folded his arms. His teacher had defeated a monster of legend. He had done the kind of thing Theo dreamt, when first he learned of magic.

"He must be very powerful," he said. His voice didn't rise. "Quite a bit more powerful than he pretended. He must be so old too. He never let on about any of this."

"Sorry, man," Hanzo said. "He doesn't tell new apprentices. It encourages them to take dumb risks and gets them killed. He asked us not to mention it when you came in case you tried to bite off more than you could chew. He said you were likely to."

"I suppose that's fair. I have a habit of that. Do you know how he beat the creature?"

Sadhbh shook her head. "He's never told us."

"But he's the only one you've ever heard doing it?"

"Yes."

"Interesting," he said. His leg spasmed once under the table. "I've not spoken to him in months. Months and months. Maybe years if you're counting in real-time. It would be nice to hear those stories from him, once I wean myself off the old thaumaturgical teat. Once I get settled somewhere. It could easily be here. This *künefe* is terrific."

"I'll bet it is," said Sadhbh, smiling.

The visit wound to a close. They scheduled their next meeting with Theo and left him with extra money and some small gifts. A toiletry kit with scented soap. A portable battery for his phone. A harmonica. They said their goodbyes and departed down alleyways, Regarding this place as like the next one they were visiting. Another place with another charity case.

Fifteen minutes later, he was outside the Diyarbakır train station. He would get the train from there to Ankara and then to Istanbul. He could be in Berlin in a matter of a few days. Yet, his thoughts boiled as he stared at the golden letters upon the station's entrance.

Gabriel had kept so much from him. He never told Theo about the importance of education in magic, the use of psychedelics, or even the effects of indulging the senses. He hadn't brought up even the mere existence of spirits. Worst of all, he had hidden the possibility of dissolution. He never told him this might happen to him. He had never warned him.

The hero had kept so much from him. The hero he wanted to be.

Well, he would face him, and demand to know why. He wouldn't be weak.

Theo left the train station. He went to a supermarket and wasted his money on a bottle of expensive wine. He needed the alcohol to confront the whispers, he told himself, as the twitches started to grow once more. He downed the bottle, drinking so fast he couldn't taste it. Then he dug out his old phone and hunted down the old number.

Hi Gabe. We need to meet.

The response was as quick as it had always been.

Ok. Can u do Accra?

Yes. Be right there.

Chapter Fourteen

There are two ways to slide easily through life: to believe everything or to doubt everything. Both ways save us from thinking.

——*Alfred Korzybski, Manhood of Humanity*

Theo landed in Accra, Ghana, where the heat choked the air out of him. He made his way into the heart of the city, to a diner Gabriel had indicated. The streets were loud. Taxis marked by yellow fenders bustled past low rows of pastel-coloured houses and billboards selling prayers. The air before him shimmered. He decided it was the heat.

As he walked, his phone lit up with messages from the others.

Hey, we're here now. How far away are you?

Yo, are you okay, man? Why aren't you replying?

Theo. Please tell us you didn't teleport.

He turned his phone off.

Gabriel awaited him at a table outside. He looked just as Theo remembered. Same leather jacket, same shaved head and rose tattoo. He had already ordered plates of jollof rice with fried tilapia for them both. Above him the sky was a monotonous grey. An empty slate, stretching on forever.

When he saw Theo, he got up and gave him a big hug.

"*Bon bini*," he said. "I hear you've become excellent at magic."

Theo was taken aback. He wanted to start the conversation more aggressively.

"I've been doing alright," he managed. He took his seat. His arm twitched.

The rice was a golden mix of yellow peppers, chilli, and coriander. The rich smell of tomato and garlic wafted off his plate.

"Have you had Ghanian jollof?" Gabriel asked, sitting down with him. "Or maybe the Nigerian version? They have a rivalry about it. It's a small thing. I can't teleport to Nigeria anymore. My mind thinks of the country, and I think about Ghanian jollof instead. I found this diner following one of those mistakes. A very happy accident, I think. I bet you're tired of McDonald's, eh?"

"You know, you never told me I should eat generic food to help my magic. Sadhbh had to tell me."

Gabriel laughed, "It's true. I never did. But even if it is not the healthiest, life needs a little soul food. This is much better than the processed supermarket stuff, or the things restaurants were throwing out."

"Maybe it is, but I don't want it."

Gabriel's easy expression fell away. He stuck his hands in his pockets.

"I see how it is. Okay then. Tell me Theo, do you have friends? Be honest."

"Yeah, sure. The enclave."

"Oh? You call them your friends?"

"What else would they be?"

Gabriel tossed his phone out onto the table. The screen lit up, showing a text from Sadhbh.

"Friends don't run out on friends," he said. "They're worried sick about you. They want to know if I've seen you."

"Have you seen me?"

Gabriel inclined his head. "No, not yet. Depending on how this goes, maybe I have. It's up to you."

"Okay." Theo drummed his fingers across the table, idly toying with his knife and fork. "I don't know why you're asking me about friends. You're the one who told me I can't get close to people."

"If I did, then I gave you the wrong idea."

"Yes, well, there's a lot of things you failed to communicate to me. How old are you, really?"

Gabriel sighed. "I am 127 years old."

"Why did you not tell me that?"

"Because you were already doing enough hero worship. It's difficult to tell someone everything they need to hear when they don't know how to listen." Gabriel gestured at the table. "You really should try the jollof by the way. Don't let it go cold. I would hate it if we do all the talking and then you never have a taste."

"Are you trying to keep me here?"

"Hah. I think I'll need more than nice food for that, don't you?"

As if to defy him somehow, Theo grabbed a fork and shoved a bite into his mouth. The jollof was comfort food, through and through. Warm, nourishing, and suffused with delicious aromas. It had been prepared by a person who loved their craft. Once Theo started eating, Gabriel tucked into his own with gusto, savouring each mouthful, cleansing his palate with lemonade to enjoy each forkful anew. Theo watched him in disbelief.

"How can you do that?" he asked. "Aren't you afraid of getting stuck?"

"No," Gabriel said, wiping his mouth. "I'm not."

"But then how? Is there some secret?"

"There's never any secret, Theo. Not really. You should know this by now. Let me ask you something. Do you remember what I asked you before I brought you to the others?"

The hair on the back of Theo's neck rose. "No clue. Bring on your lecture."

"No lecture. I only want to know if you've figured out what magic is for."

Theo shrugged. "Free air travel."

"No. Don't do jokes. Not this time."

"Okay, fine. I think it's a trick question and there's no answer. What's magic for? I mean, what is *anything* for? Nothing has a purpose. There's no grand teleology to anything. There's no point. Maybe I once thought there was a reason for me getting magic, but whatever that was, it's long gone now. Merely a flight of fancy. Is that what you wanted me to understand? Because I get it now. Message received. God is dead and blah de blah blah."

Gabriel shook his head. "That is exactly the wrong view. It is true that it's childish to think there are things like fate or destiny or heroes. Life will always contain boredom and misery and other unpleasantness. This is true. But it's childish too to think that nothing matters, or there's nothing to care about. It's the other side of the same incorrect thought. No matter what, things will matter to you. They'll be meaningful to you. You don't have a choice in that because you will pay attention to things, and your attention will create that meaning. Magic lets you expand your attention. It lets you see how similar many things are, and so you can ignore minor details. When you ignore them, you can see the things behind the things. You can see what's truly there. Then, when you find something that you want to care about, you can focus on it properly. You can see the thing for itself. Magic is for finding the things you love, for finding the things you want to love."

As he listened, Theo grew more and more disgusted until he finally snapped. "Don't get so fucking sentimental with me. I cannot handle any of your preaching right now. You obviously know what's been happening to me since you've been getting info from the others. I'm losing control of my body. I hear and see things that aren't there. I shout at nothing. I had one thing going for me in my life. One damned bloody thing in my fucking shitshow of a life and now I can't do that anymore because I did it too much and because you never fucking warned me. *Nobody* warned me. Nobody cared to, because fuck Theo right, he's just this arrogant presumptuous pretentious dirty fucking prick so let's just leave him to ruin himself so he can't sleep and he can't think and he can't fucking see out of his eyes and then he'll be dependent and ashamed and useless as he should be and we'll teach him a lesson. I bet you've been in contact with the others the whole bloody time, having a right good laugh about what's been happening to me, because you set me up for this."

The heat inside Theo sprang up like a plume of ashes, stinging his eyes.

"Theo..." Gabriel stared in shock. "I'm so sorry. I didn't know you felt this way. I had no idea you were having trouble until the others texted me. I'm so sorry. I promise you I didn't know."

Theo wiped his eyes. "Nah. Nah, nah, nah, I won't hear your pity on this. No excuses. You, apparently, are some magnificent monster-slayer who knew all about stuff like this. So, I'm not here for a parable or a nice plate of rice. I need you to tell me how to fix this. Because if anyone knows, it's you."

"I wish I knew a lot more, chief."

"Stop calling me chief!"

Gabriel rubbed his mouth in thought, "And I wish Buddhism had more to say about self-hate."

"What the fuck is that supposed to mean?"

"It means you have the problem backwards. It's not that you've cut all your sympathetic ties. If it was even possible, you would be dead. The problem is you lack sympathy for yourself. I can see it now in your face, in the way you walk. It gave you power, didn't it? You felt free because you thought nobody cared about you, you included? But there's a big difference between being without ego and trying to kill your ego. The latter is an act of hate, and hatred never ceases through hatred. Not in this world anyway.

"I'm sorry we didn't meet sooner. I didn't imagine this would happen. I think maybe you would have been much happier if I'd never approached you. Please, forgive me."

"But..." Theo struggled to reply. "But how do I heal, then?"

"You need to rest. No more, no less. Make friends, play at something without a goal. Eat good food. I don't know. All I really know is that you *must* give up magic. Whatever else, you have to stop." Gabriel pointed to the rose tattoo on his neck. "I gave myself this tattoo when I worried it would happen to me. It draws some attention. Keeps me grounded. Sadhbh dyes her hair white for the same reason. Maybe you could do the same kind of thing? It got harder for me to move around, and my skill with objects is almost gone. There are some things I miss or would like to do but can't. But maturity is when you learn to accept the people you can't be."

Theo sat with that for a while, listening to the blare of the traffic nearby. He thought about the journey he took with Gabriel and all the praise the man had received from all the other mages. He thought about how much he had looked up to him. He thought about how much hurt he had felt, knowing his teacher had let him down. How betrayed he felt.

He thought about Gabriel's remark about hero worship. About how he had regarded him.

Theo, consciously or otherwise, decided then that rather than the messiness and uncertainty Gabriel offered him, the feeling of betrayal was the truth. It was a fact, like the premise of an argument. With that fact in mind, a new analysis of his mentor snapped into place.

"You know what I think, Gabriel?" Theo whispered. "I think you're feeding me a lot of bollocks."

Gabriel blinked. "What?"

"How did you kill the Place-Eater? You did kill one, didn't you?"

"I survived one. I didn't kill one."

"You're lying to me. Sadhbh said you killed one."

"No. No magician can kill one. I don't know what she said, but that can't be true."

"I think I've figured out your scheme, professor. I think you're a very clever bastard, in fact. You don't help out with the grunt work the others do, because you're off training magicians, right? Well, there's a neat little loophole you get to exploit there, isn't there? By training new magicians, by having all these novices look up to, you get others to Regard you as powerful, so you *are* powerful. I think that's really how you keep your shit together—"

"Theo—"

"You find newbies. You Gandalf all over them. They love you. They think you're amazing. Then they all chat among themselves and spread rumours about you. They talk you up. Make you an icon. This lets you carry on eating what you want and dressing how you like. That's how you became strong enough to defeat one of those monsters. Christ, even your name means 'warrior.'"

"Theo. Stop. You know that's not how magic works."

"I'll bet you know where one of these monsters are right now. Tell me how you defeated yours, and I can do the same thing. I'll keep your scheme quiet. I'll even add to your myth, since you taught me. We can both be powerful."

"No!" Gabriel slammed his fist onto the table. "I will tell you *nothing*. Not one word. If I tell you a single thing, you'll hear it and go out and you will die. I won't encourage you. Please, you're already losing yourself. You can't pursue one. It will kill you."

Theo shot up from the table. "Fine. If you won't be any help, then I'll do it on my own. I'll kill it. I'm willing to sacrifice more than you." He swept his arm across the table, knocking the food to the ground. "And fuck you for trying to buy me over with this."

"Tell me another way to help you and I will. Please, Theo. What do you need? Why won't you stop?"

Gabriel called out the questions, but Theo was already leaving. With his master's voice in his wake, the younger mage was reminded of all the times in his life when he needed to escape from people. All the times he'd been excited to show himself and been told not to. The times he'd tried to be polite, to offer himself, only to be told to shut up and stay quiet, to stay still. But he had been the cosmos before, and he would be the cosmos again.

The next door he took brought him back to Berlin. He would begin his hunt there, with a thrill coursing down his spine, and the entirety of the world at his disposal.

He tossed his phone into a bin.

Chapter Fifteen

*The world must be ro-
manticised ... By giving
the commonplace an ele-
vated meaning, the ordi-
nary a mysterious appear-
ance, the known the digni-
ty of the unknown, the fi-
nite an infinite appearance,
I romanticise it.*

—*Novalis, Fragments*

*Man must be everyday, or
he will not be at all.*

— Henri Lefebvre, Critique
of Everyday Life

O ne month later, hungover, with dried spit at the corners of his mouth, Theo found his monster. It was in an Irish ghost estate. Beyond a chain-link fence and yards of knotweed-cracked cement lay the remains of a housing bubble: rows of identical homes that lay incomplete and inert, awaiting deliverance to tax-avoidant vulture funds. Ghost homes. Fallow structures which bred the kind of beast he hunted.

In Irish, they were *eastát na Sí*. The estate of the Fairy.

He knew it was here. He could feel it in the drifts of newspaper and empty packets on the wind, the breeze-blocks pinning down rain-leached tarpaulin. The bleached tape across the dusty windows. The beast was here, in the borders that signalled, demarcated, and sealed off life, but was not itself living.

He could feel the beast as if it was his own skin.

Beside him lay his canvas bag, laden with tools. Cans of spray paint, a Swiss army knife, a ring of keys made from various metals. A canister of kerosene. Minor pieces of driftwood. His right hand gripped a sledgehammer. His left, an empty shoulder of whiskey. His head ached.

They told him selfhood is the payment for power.

Well, he'd prove them wrong. And if not, no harm done.

He threw his materials over the fence, and then he began to climb.

The estate was quieter than it had any right to be. Even the noises from the lone road nearby felt muffled. The place smelled of nothing but rain. Theo's emotions gnarled within him, like the wood of an injured tree.

He decided he felt nothing.

He sized up the houses, trying to determine the beast's location. He was not sure what he was looking for. He knew only that there was a wrongness infiltrating his bones—the shapeless dread of an accident yet to be detailed.

There was nothing for it. He would have to draw the monster out.

He walked up to a house and pissed on it. Then he picked up a rock from a barren garden and lobbed it through a window. With his sledgehammer, he smashed through drain pipes, knocked over nearby barricades, and cracked awnings. With his knife, he scratched his own sigils into the plaster, changing each between the houses so as to distinguish them. One house received letters of the alphabet, another, smiley faces, while a third bore crude recollections of alchemical symbols.

If the Place-Eater subsisted on similarity, then he would starve it.

Every time Theo inflicted new damage on the estate, he listened, twitching. Shaking.

He heard nothing.

He crafted new insults for the beast. He tore chunks out of lawns with a found trowel, and littered the streets with gravel and soil. He broke down doors of houses and opened pipes wherever he saw them. He slashed hallways in bright spurts of blue and red spray paint until he disoriented himself with toxic fumes.

He continued the hunt like a man possessed.

As he laid waste to the beast's domain, his mind pulsed and frayed further. The whispers flooded his ears, calling him by his name, and he would shout his replies at the heavens. He would halt halfway through smashing the pavement, seeing half-images of the enclave. His emotions cavorted, like starlings in the sky.

He tried fire next. He splashed kerosene onto the frame of a front door. The smell hurt his head. He emptied the can half-out, more than enough for thick tongues of flame.

Then, when he turned, he saw it, and recognised it.

Its body had never been a body. It had never been a point of blackness. It was a lens, filling up Theo's vision. A hyperbolic distortion of space, which magnified its centre and pushed the houses to the periphery where their forms bled out into a grey rim. The centre magnified what was behind it to the point of opacity. To where nothing could be made out. It was a dark, impenetrable core, a little bigger than a person, whose geometry streaked out into the periphery with black lines. A sketching of wings, haloed in the light that they deflected away.

It moved towards him, and the shadows twisted. He caught glimpses of something within the core. A figure wearing clothes of charcoal-black, with a thin, slumped body. When the darkness moved, two headlamp eyes stared out at him.

When it spoke, he felt its voice deep within him.

Who are you?

"You think you're funny, don't you?"

You think you're funny, don't you?

"Are you mocking me?"

Are you mocking me?

Theo took two steps forward.

And all the light in the world disappeared.

Theo found himself in one of the empty rooms of the estate. The shadow was sprawled in the corner, in a puddle of tenebrous vomit and urine. It was dressed in the clothes he'd worn in Berlin. The sour stink of thrown-up vodka couldn't be mistaken.

You are an alcoholic. You started when you were young. You drank
to remove loneliness. You drank to feel mature. You drank because it
was easy comfort. You drank so much it scared your peers. You failed
your secondary school exams because you were drunk. You drowned
your potential in fermented sugars.

Is this who you are?

"Is that it? You're going to call me names? You're not getting to me
that easily."

You're not getting to me that easily.

The air shifted, and all at once Theo knew something was deeply
wrong. He couldn't identify the issue, which was that he no longer
remembered large portions of his life. Any time he'd ever drank alcohol
had been lost from his mind. Whole months, extracted like teeth. A
dread coiled in his hollowed stomach, but he didn't know what was
wrong.

The walls contorted. The hyperbolic shadow grew. When it reced-
ed, they were outside.

The night was black, starless. Streetlamps glared white in place of
the moon. Theo saw another shadow facing the closed door of his
family home, with umbral duplicates of his belongings. The house
was a small but traditional English country house, and yet somehow
it seemed to fit seamlessly into the estate.

He recognised the moment as a depiction of his eighteenth birth-
day.

Your parents didn't love you. You weren't what they wanted. You
blew up toilets at school to get attention. You stole cars. You never
stopped talking. Your teachers and your parents only knew to hurt you
for it. You were never given what you needed. You will never learn why.

Is this who you are?

"I'm a magician now," Theo growled at himself. "This is all in the past. It's irrelevant."

It's irrelevant!

The air shifted once more. Theo could no longer remember his childhood.

Theo snatched his bag up and ran to the house across the street. He doused the entryway with the rest of the kerosene and threw a match. The flames cut through the blackness. The shadows seemed all the starker. His copy watched him as he ran to a second house, where he doused the entryway with the rest of the kerosene and threw a match. The flames cut through the blackness. The shadows seemed all the starker. Then he ran to a third house, where he doused the entryway with the rest of the kerosene and threw a match.

The flames cut through the blackness.

The shadows seemed all the starker.

When he had set fire to the whole estate, Theo stopped, dripping with sweat.

Then the air shifted again, and all the fire leapt into the sky, where it became the sun.

The two of them were back in the middle of the street. Nothing had changed.

You're an ordinary person. You have no unique insights. You have no hidden strengths. You have no insurmountable flaws. Your life is your life alone, shaped by cause and effect. You receive no special love and no special hatred. You are not nothing. You are nothing more than everyone else.

Is this who you are?

"Th-this..." Theo stammered. "I was... I was... I know my life was building up to something. Please. I am more than this."

I am more than this.

This was the end of Theo.

The beast broke down Theo's mind first. It showed him friendless. It showed him alone and cold and pathetic. It showed him as stupid, obstinate, cowardly, self-righteous, and self-absorbed. It showed him all of his mistakes, every memory he would rather forget. It showed him the warnings he neglected, every second chance he had failed to use. For the Place-Eater seeks the things people cannot tolerate about themselves, and when they fail to accept them, the Eater consumes them.

Theo's shame melted him like acid.

When the beast had broken down his mind, it began to break down his body. It showed him his moles, his scars, his discolourations, and for each and every one he couldn't accept it would remove them, taking a bite out of his skin. It took blood and flesh and pumped it to its grisly periphery. It showed him his hair, greasy and receding, and took it, leaving him smooth and bald. It showed him his misaligned jaw and broke it for him. It took his red-veined nose, leaving his face smooth and fleshy. It took his fatty stomach, hidden behind thick layers, and left his trunk a scarecrow spine stringing together spindly limbs.

It took the blood and flesh, and sent it to the periphery of its body. When the beast had satiated itself, it showed him what he was, with all the things he could not accept about himself removed. What he saw was a horror, a half-thing unfit for life.

The Place-Eater removed that too.

Theo never considered himself a vagrant, even after he learned how to teleport. He had continued to believe what he needed to believe, even when life caught him looking and came for him. When next a bitter wind blew through the estate, it swept up the magician's dust, and spread it across the globe. No amount of sympathy would bring it back. Only his own could have ever done that.

About the author

Eóin Dooley (he/him) is a writer from central Ireland. Having completed a master's in cognitive science and philosophy, he turned to creative fiction, primarily to stave off a PhD. This appears to be working. His previous work can be found in Elegant Literature, Manawaker Studio, and Solar Press, with nonfiction forthcoming in Red Futures. [His urban fantasy novella, No Sympathy, is forthcoming with Android Press.] His mastodon handle is @eoindooley@mastodon.ie.

OTHER TITLES CURRENTLY AVAILABLE
AND ON PRE-ORDER FROM

Android Press
Science Fiction & Fantasy Punks
www.android-press.com

Milton Keynes UK
Ingram Content Group UK Ltd.
UKHW051602280924
448939UK00010BA/120